Susannah Indigo

Oysters Among Us

erotic tales of wonder

West Emerald Press
Boulder
Colorado
2001

West Emerald Press
westemeraldpress.com
Boulder, CO

ISBN 0-9704677-2-9

Indigo, Susannah.
Oysters Among Us.

WEST EMERALD PRESS – FIRST EDITION

Printed in the United States of America

Cover art © C.L. Wilson
      http://www.erotic-fine-arts.com/

Acknowledgments

My thanks to so many editors whose kindness and enthusiasm for my words made things possible—Louise Bacquero, Marianna Beck, Bill Brent, Susie Bright, Tom Deerfield, Jack Hafferkamp, Brian Peters, Marcy Sheiner, Greg Wharton, and Cathy Winks. My thanks also to the entire staff of Clean Sheets Magazine (www. cleansheets.com), along with all of our readers, who keep me in the writing zone day and night.

Profound appreciation flows to friends whose kind words throughout time meant everything—Michael Braverman, Diane Fisher, Jerry Forshey, Frank Koughan, Alan McDonald and every member of Z. Thanks go also to Helen Galloway, for her generosity in reading every word and critiquing from a very unique perspective.

A final note of unending gratitude to my dear friend and master editor, Jeff Beresford-Howe, for the sparks and the laughter, the sharing of crazy ideas for so many years, and the belief that turned out to be true.

Contents

Oysters Among Us

Flying Through China

*T*he tea-light candles are tiny and white and encased in gold. "Light six of them at a time," Jack said when he gave them to me. "Six is the sacred number of Aphrodite, the goddess of love." I laugh when he says things like that, but I listen. "Bathe in salted water scented with roses, China my love," he said, "like a gentle ocean bath, and imagine that the water is the sacred fluid that will endow you with all the powers of love." He gave me tiny packets of bath oil filled with rose petals, but somehow he forgot the salt. Morton provides that from the cupboard—iodized, of course.

The candlelight flickers on the ceiling as I drop my robe and lower myself into the steaming water, pretending that he is here watching me while I practice. After our first night together I told him I would try everything for him. That was the night when he touched a part of me that I had thought was lost. He took me to his loft and removed the clips from my long hair and began to dance with me. He lit candles all around the room and danced me to the end of the night. I wanted to be a dancer when I was a little girl, but somehow never followed through on that dream. Jack brought out secrets in me, he whispered to me of the magic of tantric sex, and then he had me blow out all the candles but one and made love to me slowly while I wrapped my legs around him and sat on his lap on the hardwood floor.

"I will try everything for you," I whispered when we woke up the next morning—surprising myself with the words, with the wetness between my legs just from looking at him, and with my desire to climb up on top of him while he was still asleep. "Wanton" is not a word anyone ever used to describe me. "Yes, you will, China," was all that he said then. I just had no idea where he'd make me start.

There are so very many things I've never tried in my life: I've never worn a corset, I've never eaten a truffle and I've never touched another woman sexually. I had no idea that I wanted any of these things until I moved to the town of Boulder and met Jack and then made friends with Annie Braverman and her partner Sam. Annie has a closet that makes me blush.

I slide my hands under the water and feel the curve of my hips and the hardness of my thighs. I look at my body through Jack's eyes, watching my nipples grow hard and rise above the water. I've had these large nipples ever since I was a teenager, and I used to be so embarrassed by how they'd poke out against everything and grow hard from the touch of the material.

"You will learn to go topless around the house, China," Jack said, "especially when we're cooking. There is nothing better." I could think of a couple of better things, like aprons, but cooking is the height of sensuality to me and I'm good at it. I used to read books by M.F.K. Fisher when I was a teenager, and she wrote all those sensual things about food and hunger and for all I know maybe she did because she went topless, I don't know. *Yes,* I said to Jack, and *yes,* and *yes.* I feel like Molly Bloom when I'm around him. *Yes. Yes.* I seem to be saying this to him all the time. But I want what he has. *Yes.*

My pussy hair is full and pale red, just like my very long hair that I always keep in a braid or tied up so that nobody notices it. Jack is always taking it down. He loves that I've hung onto that part of me from my strange childhood, and he loves that I've kept my name. My full name is China Sunflower Thomas. One read of this name and people can almost guess what year I was born. My parents lived on a commune and were never married—at least not to each other. A hundred times I've considered changing my name, but have never gotten around to it. My childhood only made me turn out conservative—I'm an accountant and live in a proper condo in the foothills of Boulder. I hide my long, wavy hair in a bun for work. I pay my bills on time, I read serious fiction, I go to church.

"But you're only twenty-six years old," Jack laughed when I told him these things. "You've forgotten to live." I looked at him sitting in my office as I sorted out his messy financial affairs when he had the nerve to say that to me. I wanted to smack him, but, looking at him, I flashed on my childhood at the Grand Lake Cooperative and suddenly I couldn't say a word. Long hair, knowing eyes and a great beard. A free spirit. He was definitely not my type. The only problem was that as he sat across from me at my desk and humbled himself to my calculator, I found myself crossing my legs to try to ignore the fact that just by looking at me he was making me wet.

In the candlelight of my bathroom none of it seems to matter. The only thing that's important is that I learn to bring myself to orgasm with my own hands, no vibrator, no man; that I keep stroking my clit in this way that feels so right, that I close my eyes and learn how to lose myself enough so that I can do this in front of Jack some day. "Sex is all about the transference of power," he told me, and somehow I knew he was not talking about my Hitachi Magic Wand and the electrical outlet in my bathroom.

"When you master this first challenge, China, we can start down the path to the secrets of high sex." I want the secrets and I want the touch that I have right this second that makes me know I am indeed related to the goddess of love in some very distant way, and I want to smell like roses and see the flicker of tea-lights in my dreams every single night.

And of course I want to do all this before Jack comes over at eight, and Annie and Sam arrive for dinner.

I do not cook topless. Nor do I wear a corset that pushes my breasts up to the sky. I do skip my bra and wear a soft cashmere sweater that matches my hair, and I know that my nipples will stand out for Jack sometime during the evening and this will make him happy.

"Take your hair down," Jack murmurs with the first kiss of my neck. When I hesitate, he takes the clip out of my hair, and I find I am enjoying this game of deciding how we will arrange my hair every time we greet. When he comes over he brings me roses, pale orange roses that he says look like me, sometimes a single rose, sometimes two dozen; he brings music; he brings wine; but mostly he brings so very many kisses. I started having sex on the commune when I was thirteen, but somehow the art of kissing and flirting and teasing got lost in the mix of free love and the constant nudity that embarrassed me every single day and the birth-control my mother handed to me at fourteen.

Jack kisses me, he just kisses me, and I want to take more than my hair down and climb up and into this man and stay warm forever. Maybe it's the way his beard feels against my cheek, maybe it's the way his tongue is exploring every inch of my mouth, maybe it's the feel of his hard cock up against my jeans or maybe I'm just turning into a slut.

"Let's cook," he says with a smile, pulling away from me. "The wait is always worth it."

Easy for him to say. For all I know, he can probably just light one single tea-light candle, turn on the hot water for his bath, touch himself and come before he even gets to the cold water. I think I'll ask him about this someday, if I can ever find the words. Words about sex rarely cross my tongue. When he talked about masturbating, I told him, "I can't even say that word, I hate it," and I even hated having to admit this to him. "That's cool, China," he said. "We'll just call it something else. Let's call it 'flying,' because sometimes it almost is."

When Annie Braverman enters a room the light shifts. She's ten years older than I am, but she has an air of eroticism around her that makes me envious. She wears long flowing skirts and leotards and beaded earrings that dangle down below her chin, but she's not exactly pretty in any conventional way. She has a basic natural Colorado kind of look, with long dark brown hair, or actually "espresso" colored hair as she told me once, direct from the bottle. She says she used to be a blonde once and hints at having quite a past, but I can't imagine Annie anywhere but right here and now bringing energy to this room. Her lover Sam lives in San Francisco and is tall and dark and Jewish and seems smarter than anyone else I know, but he is still a bit of a mystery to me. I do so like to watch when he looks at Annie like she's his own personal angel just come down from heaven.

"I brought you strawberries, China," Annie says, "dipped in white chocolate." Even her food offerings seem sexual.

Jack and I finish cooking and leave Annie and Sam

in charge of the music and the wine. I only blush a little when Jack can't find the salt and I have to sneak into the bathroom for it. Annie talks at dinner about her two adopted kids. "Raising these kids to be capable of joy and laughter and intimacy, that's my thing," she says. "My other passions right now are . . . let's see: Red Rocks at sunrise, struggling to learn aikido, helping people through my work, feta cheese omelets, hot-air balloons, and poetry."

Sam puts his arm around her and raises his eyebrows. "Of course, Sam, too — goes without saying," she says. "It's Sam's eyes that I love the most." She reaches to kiss him and there's a level of intensity in the way their eyes lock and know and smile and I can barely stand it.

When they finally break apart, Annie turns to Jack. "You know, I think everyone should know their passions and keep them in focus. How about you Jack, what are your passions?"

"Passions? I guess I'd say making my pictures, making love, making connections. And then — snowboarding at Winter Park, good jazz, China. And baseball."

At least I come before baseball. Man I hope she doesn't ask me this question. What could I say — making money? getting to work on time? filing 1040s? alphabetizing my bookshelves?

"How about you, China? I love knowing this about my friends."

Only Annie can ask these kinds of questions without having people laugh and make jokes about it.

"Well . . . um . . . cooking . . . and, Jack." It sounds so lame.

"China's been taking flying lessons," Jack says with a smile to help me out, and I think I might kill him.

"Yeah, right — not really," I laugh and reach to kiss him instead of kill him, trying to act like Annie. "And you, Sam, what are your passions?" A master of diversion, that's me.

He's ready. I think a person would have to be ready to be with Annie. "Music. Words. Annie and her kids. Writing. San Francisco. Sushi. Leather. Four-poster beds. Brunettes. The Victoria's Secret store on Broadway. Foreign films, Rome, skiing the back bowls at Copper Mountain. Baseball . . ."

Sam is only stopped by Jack's discovery that they both love the Cubs. I have a feeling he could have gone on all night and I'm impressed.

"Yeah," I offer. " I had to entice Jack away from watching that big Cubs game tonight for this dinner."

The guys look at each other, check the clock, then eye the TV off in the corner.

Annie laughs. "Go ahead and watch the rest of it, you guys. China and I will just lock ourselves away and do girl things, like maybe try on shoes."

I sure hope she's joking, because even my shoes are boring. We pour more wine and wander off to my bedroom while the men grab the remote and hit the couch.

"So, China, what's with the flying lessons?" Annie asks as we settle in to talk. She doesn't miss much.

I break down and tell her everything. How hard all of it is for me, all the things that Jack gives me, how uptight I feel. She just smiles.

"All that sensual stuff is good for you, I think, but what do guys know? I'm an expert at flying every which way. Remember, Sam lives a thousand miles away. All you need is a woman tutor. Those who can, teach. A tutor, darlin', and then you need a good hard fantasy."

Oh man, it was hard enough coming up with passions, and now I have to dig up a fantasy?

"I don't really have any fantasies, Annie, except for Jack. But thinking about him during this just makes me nervous."

"No problem, China. I'll loan you one of my fantasies to try on. Kind of like sharing clothes, except after you try it on to see if it fits, you can keep it if you like. I'm fond of fantasies with faceless men, you know, the kind of guy you never cook with, or fight with. The kind of guy who doesn't know that the TV even *exists* while you're in the room with him."

Annie locks the door, lights the candles, turns off the lamp and lies down on the bed beside me. "Close your eyes, China."

"But the guys are out there. This takes me forever, Annie."

"It won't. Trust me. You have to find the wildness deep inside of you. I'll even join in."

I peek, and Annie is lifting her skirt next to me and it's the sexiest thing I've ever seen a woman do. She wears nothing underneath and she has no hair at all on her pussy and looks like a little girl.

"You can watch me, China, or we can put a scarf around your eyes to help you lose yourself and take off."

I want to watch. I suddenly can understand why Jack wants this. I take my jeans and panties off as she instructs and I lie back and spread my legs. She props me up with the pillows so I can see, but I notice that she has closed her eyes and is touching herself.

"There's a man," Annie says, "who has come to me after midnight almost every night of my life. He is tall and has long, very black hair. I don't know him, but I know he wants something from me and that he has to have it. He scares me sometimes. Touch yourself in any way that feels right, China, and I will tell you what he wants from you tonight."

Annie is not exactly touching me, but she is only inches

away and I swear I can feel her skin.

We lie at right angles so we can see each other. Her voice is like velvet when she says, "Don't say a word, China, just touch yourself and listen to my story."

You are lying on the beach in St. Croix and it is very hot. You're wearing a white bikini and you have a tan along with your freckles. Everybody gets a great tan in my fantasies. You are stretched out on your blue beach towel that says 'San Francisco Ballet' across it in big letters. I am there with you, but I have left to wander down the beach to find us something to drink. You lie on your back with your hat over your face, but you can still tell that suddenly your sun is gone. When you take off the hat and look up he is there, standing over you, and he is tall with pitch black hair and soft brown eyes. You know him. It's the same man you chatted with on the airplane, and who you have seen everywhere you go around town. He looks at you expectantly, and you can't help but notice that he is fully dressed here on the beach.

"I've been watching you, China," he says, and you think about moving and getting up but you don't. Instead you look around and can't figure out why there is suddenly no sun, no people, no noise, nothing except for this man staring at you.

"May I join you?" he asks sitting down right next to you, so close that he is just barely touching your skin, and you are hot all over again.

"Yes," you whisper, because what else can you say.

It begins to rain, a gentle but steady rain here on the island. All you can see is the rain and the man and he moves until he's blocking the rain from your face and he is inches away and he kisses you.

You think maybe you should get up and take this man to your room or maybe you shouldn't, but then he says "Don't move, China. I want you right here."

The rain is not cold, but his hands on your legs feel like the sun and you move into his heat. He asks you why you are wearing such bright red lipstick here on the beach and you say you don't know, but then you remember your friend Annie made you put it on, and you remember that it is called 'Scarlet Begonias' and it is the same color that she put on your fingernails and your toes. You tell him this. He runs his finger across your lips. He begins to draw down your chest with his finger and stops just above your breasts.

"Take your top off," he says, and you slip it off and arch your back for him like it is the most natural act in the world and you have known him forever. You're sure that this is what you were born for, to lie here on the white sand with rain falling all around you and a man with black hair and strong hands lying on top of you and protecting you from it all.

"Spread your legs," he says, and you move underneath him and say "yes" and you try and think of his name but it doesn't seem to matter now. "Do you want me to fuck you, China?" he asks quietly, so quietly that you think his voice is coming from somewhere out there in the rain. His hands run down from the curve of your breast over your belly and he is taking off the bottom of your bikini. He kisses you where the softness of your red pussy hair meets your wetness, just one single kiss. He lies back on top of you and you can feel his hard cock pressing into you.

You forget that you are here in the rain and that you barely know this man and that there must be other people out there somewhere and that if the rain stops they will all see you. It somehow doesn't matter because all there is in the world is the sensation of every inch of your skin pressing into his and it seems that this man belongs inside of you but somehow you have to find the words to say yes.

"Yes," you hear from somewhere in the rain, and it sounds like your voice but it is not, it's your friend Annie's voice and she is there next to you with her hands on your ankles and she is saying "yes," not to him but to you, "yes China," she says, "yes," like she is reminding you that you like to wear lipstick, and "yes," like she is reminding you that you need to let go, and "yes," like she is the only one who can tell you that you need to say yes to this man and this feeling and this place and that it is all okay and that of course this is what you want and what you need.

"Do you want me to fuck you, China?" the man asks one more time, and it is barely a question. He holds your wrists together over your head and as soon as you say "yes, fuck me" you can feel Annie's hands on your ankles and she is spreading your legs wider for him and watching. He begins to enter you, so slowly that you think you will die from the pleasure and your lack of control and then he is driving into you hard and fast and you hear Annie saying "yes" over and over and you are with her and with him and you hope everyone in the world is watching and feeling exactly what you feel.

I hear Annie moaning and coming to her own story and I am coming with her and I think maybe she really did have her hands on my ankles, but I'm not even sure where I am. It is all so amazing and I am laughing and hugging her. Real hugs, the one Jack calls the melting hug, where your whole body embraces the other person.

Annie laughs with me. "Hey, it works for me every time. Get dressed, darlin'. I think we're way past the 7th inning stretch out there."

As soon as Annie and Sam have gone for the night, I hurry to find Jack, who is in the kitchen cleaning up. I can't stand it. I turn off the water, wrap my arms around him and whisper to him.

"I need you to fuck me."

His eyes widen, but I give him credit for not laughing.

"Did I hear you right, China? Say it again."

"I need you to fuck me, Jack." I've never said that to a man before in my life. I pull my sweater off over my head and kneel in front of him and undo the belt on his jeans.

"Louder, China." I can hear the smile in his voice and I take his hard cock in my mouth and wrap the words right around it. "Fuck me, Jack. Fuck my mouth. Fuck me everywhere." I want to take him so far inside of me that I don't know who I am anymore. I'm dripping inside of my jeans and I need him there too. I feel positively . . . well, *wanton*. "God, fuck me, Jack, please fuck me, here, in the kitchen."

He is on me in a flash, and lifts me up and turns me

around and takes off my jeans and lays me across the counter. "I guess this is not the night for learning the gentle *Streaming Process*, is it, baby." His hands are hard and good on my ass and my thighs and he is spreading my legs back around his waist and wrapping me tight and all that floods my brain is *fuck me, fuck me, Jack*. My face is hard on the cold counter and he is standing behind me and when his cock slides all the way into my pussy hard and fast I begin to come, and he drives me harder and harder pulling me back against him and I know, I know, I know all the secrets of the fucking universe and he never stops until he comes so far up inside of me and reaches me in places I didn't even know were there.

When I wake up at three a.m. and reach for Jack across the bed, I know what I want. If a woman wants to come for a third, or is it fourth, time in the same night, what on earth does this make her—a nympho? just wanton? or maybe even—interesting?

Jack struggles awake as I kiss him, long and slow with my tongue deep in his mouth, the kind of kiss I forgot existed for me, and there are dark men and strange women with beaded earrings dancing in my head, but mostly there is Jack weaving through it all, waiting, smiling, surprised.

"Jack, darling . . . "

"What?" he whispers from his half-awake state. I light the two candles on the nightstand and climb back into bed and pose for him.

"Watch me now."

Snowdancing

*T*hings are not always as they seem: India ink does not come from India; rice paper is not made from rice; the Holy Roman Empire was neither holy nor Roman nor an empire. And just because I'm strapped onto this snowboard pretending to look cool and confident at the top of the Mad Hatter Run doesn't mean I know what I'm doing and wouldn't much rather be back in bed with Annie Braverman's strong legs wrapped high around my waist.

"Getting high, Sam," Annie had said to me, "that's what the three day seminar is all about. The art of high sex, skydancing, sensual massages. Learning the yoga of love, as they say."

"Snowboarding," my friend Jack had added. "Sam, you'll have to try it while we're there, it will keep you young." He'd smiled. "Plus, people will get naked on the floor all around you." So I signed up.

But Jack is young and I'm not and I'd just as soon not go down this hill without two planks on my feet and two poles for balance. Six feet three inches is a long way down to the snow. "How old would you be if you didn't know how old you really were?" is one of Annie's favorite questions. At 10,000 feet with teenagers flying past me, I'd say about sixty-two and aging fast. In bed with Annie riding me like a wave, I am seventeen. Ordinary days I show up as forty-three and try to get by.

At least the high-sex class is not here at full altitude where I can barely breathe—8,000 feet high at the hotel is bad enough. In the first session last night we breathed together a lot. We "awakened our inner voices," "saluted each others' hearts" and talked on and on about the mysteries of tantric sex. I'm not convinced yet that any of this is better than a great blow job, but I did get to see Jack's girlfriend China topless under all that gorgeous red hair. Not to mention Annie stripping down to one of those black lacy things that can make men stupid.

The snow is falling harder. I keep saying to myself over and over again like a mantra, "I know how to ski, I know how to ski." My inner voice, slightly nervous, replies, "So what? It's not related. You have to go down the hill sideways on this snowboard." Then it offers, "Don't worry, only thirty-two people a year die in skiing accidents compared to ninety-nine by lightning." My inner-voice knows way too much; I'd prefer that it stay asleep.

This is a defining moment here—in a half hour people will be getting naked all over the soft blue carpeting of the Grand Ballroom at the Top of the Rockies Hotel, and all I have to do to get there is lean into the mountain and carve the way Jack showed me. In my younger days when I was struggling and new to *The Program*, they taught me to go through life acting "as if." Act *as if* you have faith and hope, and maybe it will come. I dig as deep as I can and try to find the feeling, as if I am brave, as if I am young, as if this board will not flip me on my ass any minute, and I begin to slide down.

An hour later I make it to the ballroom, but nobody's naked yet.

"Where have you been?" asks Annie.

"Oh, I was just enjoying the view up there too much to come down."

They're all discussing today's question on the chalkboard. "Where does the white go when the snow melts?" I sigh. When you've been a journalist for twenty years you just know too many things, even things you'd rather not, and there's not a lot of magic left in the world. Last night's koan was "Does any snowflake ever fall in an inappropriate place?" I hear enough of these things and it starts sounding like Yogi Berra, saying things like, "If you don't know where you are going, you might wind up somewhere else." Baseball's easily got as much crazy-wisdom as all this Zen stuff.

Nita DeLosReyes, one of the seminar leaders, gets up and talks about snow. I'm sure this is related to sex somehow. Hopefully soon. I'd much prefer to think of anything hot rather than the snowbank I was just in.

"Get comfortable while Nita starts us off," Nita's partner Ruby says. These two seem like one of those couples who must have been born together, or met shortly after birth, the kind of couple you try to avoid unless you're madly in love yourself. Annie, whose kids go to school with their kids, is crazy about both of them.

I look around. It seems to me that "comfortable" has a lot of definitions. Some people are wearing sweats, some strip down, some just look nervous. Nita is jazzing about snowflakes and I can't help but notice that the woman wears two gold snowflake earrings pierced in each ear. I wonder what her fetish might be.

"Each of us is going to capture their own unique experience in this session," Nita says. "This afternoon we will work on touching, honoring our inner man and inner woman, and rediscovering our senses one at a time."

Annie sits back between my legs and sighs with

pleasure. She is wearing something new to make me pay attention today, a little white and blue frilly thing that covers as much of her body as a swimsuit does, but I swear it's not the same. My inner-man knows what it wants from her.

I touch Annie's shoulders. They are freckled and strong and sometimes it is enough to just touch them when she's wearing one of her sexy summer dresses. But this class may be tough for me. My grandparents came from Russia, a country that never even had a word for "sex" before they adopted the American word in this century, because they believed in showing, not telling, and in privacy. I've always believed that peoples' sex lives should not be discussed in the office, on the streets, and God knows, not in the newspaper.

Annie moves back against my belly and pulls my arms around her to hold her tight and I change my mind. Stupid *and* easy, that's me. Just the scent of her hair can make me hard. Why not do this for her? I will act as if it is quite possible that someone can teach me better ways to have sex.

"We're going to pass out some equipment," Nita says up in front. "There are small bags of honey dust with a feather-brush for each couple and one of these black satin blindfolds."

What did my grandparents know? They were pretty old anyway. Maybe they would have been right here beside me on the carpet if they lived in this new century, brushing and touching and making up new words for sex as they went, perfect words, dozens of words for sex like the Eskimos are supposed to have for snow.

My hands are over the white lace on Annie's breasts and I'd swear she slid them there. I have wanted to own Annie since the day that I met her—control her, surprise her, delight her, keep her laughing and sexy and hot—and most days I think I do, but just before dawn sometimes it occurs to me that I know who owns whom. There can be no limits here. This is what I want, this is what I need, this may be what will save me—to sit in a room skin to skin with beautiful Annie and begin to learn again.

Things are not always as they seem: the white of snow doesn't exist except as a reflection off the crystals; an ordinary scarf takes on great eroticism when you know it's a blindfold; honey dust is made from real honey but feels like silk.

"Partners," Ruby is saying, walking around the room, lighting all the candles. "We have the same choices as last night. Those who are here without a partner may practice these skills by themselves, they may double up with another single, or triple with a couple. Nita and I will work together with one of you also."

I look around the room. I had no problem saluting the heart of the pretty blond woman next to us last night. On the other hand, I may have some guy problems with this touching session. I'm afraid to look at Annie—she's a little more open and free with her body than I am. I can't imagine coming to something like this alone, but people do. There's quite a mix in the eighty people in this room—there's even an inspiring couple who look to be in their sixties. May I live to blindfold Annie when I'm old and turning gray.

"Hey Flan," Annie says to a guy that she knows from Boulder who is lounging around comfortably with his honey dust not far from us. "Come join us."

Oh, man, not Erick Flanagan. He's young. Flan wanders over to us with a smile and his long hair pulled back in a ponytail band, looking for all the world like he's just strolling around Alfalfa's, the health food store he works in. Except that when he's there, they make him wear more than red flannel boxers.

"Is it OK, Sam?" he asks. Annie's watching me, and though I think I might go alpha-male and smack him if he touches her, I act *as if* and say "sure."

The lights are lowered, there is candlelight everywhere, the music is on. At least it's not Yanni. Drumming and exotic African dance music fill the room.

We make our "sacred circle." We start the breathing together as instructed.

"Start with one person stretched out on the pillows and then take turns when it feels right," Ruby says. "Orgasms are not important here. We're going for something different. Skydancing is the ancient term for reaching an ecstatic state through many different methods. We're trying just one."

Annie goes first, stretching out like a cat, with me positioned between her legs and Flan positioned by her head. The butterfly position, Ruby calls it. Annie's hands are behind her neck, a blindfold tight around her eyes. I like watching her with some of her senses muffled. It makes me want to do more.

Flan and I begin to brush her as instructed, tiny strokes of honey dust in circles from her head to her toes. I don't look at any part of Flan except his hands, and my brain pretends they're not really attached to a guy. Annie is sighing and writhing beneath our hands. She asks me to take the white lace off her body and I do. Flanagan begins to brush her nipples and somehow it's okay. I start on her belly and there's a rhythm between us that reminds me of when I used to play in my band, the give and take, trading leads, finding the right changes.

I can hear other people sighing and it seems so right. I think I can paint Annie's body forever and then take all night and lick every speck of honey dust off.

Annie turns over on her belly, and I am spreading her legs and circling, just circling the brush around the inside of her thighs, over and over. I don't go near her pussy because we're not supposed to, but it doesn't seem to matter. The smell of the honey is overwhelming. Flan is holding her arms above her head and brushing up and down the inside of her arm and she begins to shudder. Her smile is so strong that she seems incapable of speaking. She is sighing, though, and she looks like she's in another world. I watch her body stiffen and her breath change, and if I didn't know better I'd swear that we'd just fucked.

What a great idea this all is.

Annie rests in my arms afterward and says little while Flan and I talk quietly and agree he will go next.

He stretches out on the pillows and I can feel my brain shifting. Bodies seem to be just bodies, touch is just touch, I am wise and I am open to new things. I'm fascinated by every naked person in this room. Maybe it's true that every person is born bisexual and we just rarely get around to discovering it. I know that every man in this room is hard and I seem to find that fascinating too. Sex is the most interesting thing in the world, just like it was when I was thirteen and experimenting with my boyhood friends.

Annie sits between my legs and puts my hand in hers and we begin. I catch sight of Jack and China out of the corner of my eye and I remember that once, after many beers, Jack told me that he sucked a man's cock when he was nineteen and that he liked it. We never talked about it again, but I never thought of him quite the same way. It seemed like he had a leg up on me in things sensual. Annie takes Flan's boxers off and it's all right. I'm here, in the moment, and it's all there is. Flan's body is shining with honey dust and beautiful, and looking openly at another man's erect cock turns me on. Watching Annie sit between his legs and circle around it, brushing honey dust on his belly, on his thighs and on his balls is like watching her in a dream.

We do this forever, breathing and brushing and circling, and Flan begins to do something I didn't know a man could do. He's shaking and moving and there's an electric energy passing between the three of us and he's sighing as though he just fucked Annie. I watch his cock start to go soft but he hasn't actually come, at least not the way I'm used to. I'll be damned if I don't feel as if it just might be true that there are other kinds of "whole body" orgasms in this world that I know nothing about.

Annie takes Flan's blindfold off and holds him tight for a few minutes and then hugs me.

"Your turn, Sam."

Things are sometimes more than they seem: people look entirely different in winter clothes than they do naked on blue carpeting; William Burroughs might have been right that you can simulate drugged ecstatic states; the tiny white lights around this ice rink reflect off the snow and make me sure that the white actually exists.

I'm not quite clear what all happened this afternoon, but I distinctly remember hands and more hands and the smell of honey and the combination of Annie's soft skin and Flan's callused hands transporting my mind somewhere else. I hadn't been blindfolded since I was a kid playing pin-the-tail-on-the-donkey.

"At the dance tonight by the skating rink," Nita said at the end of the session, "we want you to pay attention to all of your senses. Talk about what happened to you this afternoon and tell people how you feel."

I don't think I want to talk about it with Annie. I

want to show her.

Some people are dancing, some skate, all to the same music, which sounds suspiciously like Yanni. It is one of those perfectly clear and still Colorado nights where you barely notice the cold. Annie looks spectacular and different as always. She wears a long midnight blue velvet skirt that twirls when she dances, a baby blue sweater and her white furry boots. Her long hair is tied back on top little-girl style with a velvet ribbon. Every time I see Annie my first thought is, "What is she wearing underneath? Lace? Leather? Nothing?"

I hold her tight while we dance and I whisper. "Reach in my pocket, Annie."

She reaches into my jeans and pulls out two of the black blindfolds from this afternoon and laughs. "What?"

"I didn't turn them back in at the end of the workshop. I think we need more practice."

"We do?" she asks.

"Definitely. My kind of practice. Do you trust me, Annie?" I say, still whispering.

She smiles. "Of course. I think."

"I want to tell you what to do tonight. Working on our senses, of course. This might be sort of a sixth sense I'd like to take away for a while—your sense of control over me."

She leans into me and I whisper what I want. "Let's go for a ride on the chairlift."

"I can't go on the lift in my skirt, Sam."

"Sure you can. I'll help."

One lift runs for the few night skiers. I grab our jackets and I help Annie onto the lift, holding her skirt to the side. The lift attendant just grins at us. Maybe he was at the hotel this afternoon. It's hard to tell with clothes on.

The lift runs slowly at night and the view of the lights is breathtaking.

"Look at me, Annie."

She turns slightly toward me and I kiss her deeply.

"Now." I bring the black satin up to her eyes and wrap it around her hair and tie it tightly behind her head. She gasps and mumbles something about being scared.

"Don't be scared, I'm holding you. I'll describe everything on the way up."

"Can anyone see us, Sam?"

I look around, but all I ever see is Annie. "Probably not, baby."

I hold her close and she's very still.

"It's beautiful this way, Sam, you're right." She kisses me in that way that sends every sense I've ever had directly to my cock.

We're almost to the top of the hill and I love that she doesn't ask how she will get off without being able to see. Or maybe she thinks we're just staying on and riding back down.

I know the top of these hills, I've spent a lot of time up here recently. I lift Annie off the chair before it bends for the return downhill and set her down in the snow.

"Sam, I can't tell if anyone else is here."

"I know. Senses, Annie, senses—but without one the others are so keen. Tell me what you feel as we walk." I put my hand tight on her waist and lead her exactly to where I want her.

"I feel lost. But I can hear the snow crunching beneath my boots perfectly. I'm a little scared. And, OK, a little wet, and a little weak in my knees."

"Let's try some more senses." I lean her back against the big wooden trail map that I came to know so well earlier in the day. "Do you trust me, Annie?"

"Yes."

I pull out the other blindfold and use it to tie her hands behind her back.

"No touch. Now all you have to do is stand real still for me."

I lift her long blue skirt to find only a wisp of blue lace covering her pussy and I kiss it.

"Oh god, Sam."

"Yes."

I can still taste traces of honey dust everywhere and it all mixes in with the taste of lace and the taste of Annie and my tongue goes for it all. I let her skirt fall down over me, and all I can think is that I would kill for one of those ski-photographers—who are always wanting to snap your photo when you're fumbling down the hill — to come by and snap this picture of a beautiful woman blindfolded with her hands behind her back writhing against the trail map while I work on driving her wild under her skirt.

I spread her legs with my hands and drive my tongue in and out, pausing to kiss and suck her clit, listening to her moan, not even caring myself who's around. Annie coming to the force of my tongue is the highest sex I know, and when she does I am there holding her tight and feeling her passion all the way down through my toes.

She's kissing me again and I know she wants more and I know what she needs.

"Turn around, Annie."

I untie her hands from behind and re-tie them around the trail post, bending her over from behind and lifting her skirt again.

"Ask me to fuck you, Annie. Right here in the snow where anyone can come by and see you like this. Maybe Flan is watching. Maybe our whole class is here. Tell me you love it."

She barely pauses, wiggling her ass against my hard cock. "God, yes, Sam. Please fuck me right here."

Blue velvet in my hands, breaths coming harder and shorter at the heights of altitude and passion, entering the only place I know that feels like home, coming into Annie so hard and so fast that I begin to lose track of where I am.

We sit together on a tree stump for a long time afterward, Annie on my lap whispering in my ear, satin scarves off, hands locked together behind my neck anyway. We come back to our senses slowly, and I notice that we sit at the top of the Mad Hatter Run. Seems to me as if I was up here once before.

But I was so much older then. I'm younger than that now.

Blue Rooms

"*I* think it speaks well of my life that I don't spend the whole day on AOL, Erick Flanagan," Ruby says pointedly as she passes the butternut squash risotto across the table to Nita.

I suppose this is true, but it makes me wonder. Just how many hours can you spend on AOL before your life is poorly regarded? What's the cut-off point? Twenty minutes a day? A whole hour, downloaded mail included? And would this include all seven IDs, or could each one be spoken badly of on its own?

Ruby is my much-older cousin, twice removed by light years of experience and smarts. She's a therapist and a lesbian who is joined at the hip with her partner Nita in a way that often makes people want to ask her the secret of true love. She's good at cooking, bad at answering her e-mail, and very good at giving me a hard time about my life whenever she gets the chance. Kind of like the big sister I never had. And maybe never wanted.

"I don't spend that much time online," I mumble into my wine glass, and I wonder if anyone ever admits it when they do.

To tell you the truth, Ruby, I consider saying, I spent six

hours in a chat room called *YoungMan SeeksHotOlderWomen* on Tuesday night. I met at least two women that I expect to get to know better through email, eventually meet, respect and then fuck. It speaks well of my life, I think, Ruby, that nowadays I stay out of sleazy bars and instead sit in my boxers at my keyboard by candlelight and explore my sexuality by exchanging words with women so wet you think you can smell them through the screen. It's true, Ruby, that I often keep a window open into the chat room called *ColoradoMen4Men,* but I'm honest with all the women; and OK, it's true that most nights I eat a dinner of peanut-butter-crackers or your delicious leftovers right there at my desk; and yes, it's true that I have seven different IDs, which is a little schizoid, but at least I use one of them to correspond with relatives like you, Ruby. And yes, it's true that although I'm only twenty-four years old and pretty inexperienced with women, tonight at midnight I'm going to the Oxford Hotel to meet a woman who's more than ten years older than me, a woman who I know only as Isis. Isis is going to be blindfolded when I enter her room and will never even see my face as we play out our scripted fantasy of the stranger in the night who gives her exactly the kind of kinky sex she's craving.

"Pass the squash," is all I actually say. I'm going to need plenty of energy tonight.

"Right, sweetie, you're never online." Ruby laughs. "I tried to call you a million times the other night and got nothing but a busy signal. I'd like to think you were on the phone to Boston with your mom, but I know better."

I gotta' get a second phone line.

It's true that I may not call my own mother much, but I did get her online to help keep her busy in her retirement. One day I met her on AOL—using ID FLANAGAN24, of course: the well-behaved one—to show her how to navigate the chat rooms. I even taught her how to create a private room so she can talk with her grandkids whenever she wants. I gave her specific instructions, but it took a while. When she arrived in the private room I'd made, she typed, "That's strange, Erick, all the rooms I see are blue." I told her how to adjust the color on her monitor but she didn't seem to understand what I was saying. Then halfway through the conversation I realized what she meant: "blue" as in obscene, profane, indecent. In her old-fashioned way she was trying to say that she was shocked by all the sexual chat room names I'd led her past on AOL.

Blue rooms. That's where I spend my time, the bluer the better. I can't help it—I get an intense high from making a sexual connection through my words and thoughts. Girls wouldn't look at me twice when I was in high school; most guys wouldn't either, come to think of it. I was a lonely, weird, confused kid with only one friend. I didn't know how to reach out to anyone else, and I guess that now I'm making up for lost time.

Most of the women I chat with live far away. Most of them, I never meet. They may not even be who and what they say they are. It doesn't matter to me, though I do try to take care not to run into people like Ruby, or God help me, my mother. There ought to be a neon sign appearing on the screen when you log on that reads, "Everybody is here for different reasons, and that's cool." Some women I just like to talk to, some I try to avoid after a while, and some I connect with so hard and so fast that there's no question that my future is . . . rising. There's only one thing that they all have in common: They all talk to me about sex within the first five minutes. Where else on earth can you do this?

The first woman from AOL that I met face-to-face was named Cassady, Cassady from Chicago. She was fascinated by my sexual tales from the first moment we chatted right up until that night I met her in Vail and tried to fulfill her fantasy—that I would fuck her exactly as though she were a man.

Cassady's profile read—"HOTCASS: femme/ married with kids/short blonde hair/ 38/ slim/ professional/sexuality often undetermined/kinkier than thou."

My own read—"FLAN4U: male/single/bi/24/long-haired/rock-climbing snowboarder/into extreme sports and extreme sex."

In some weird way we were a match.

There are people who think about sex day and night and there are people who do not. Since nobody wears tags in real life, it's damned hard to tell who's who. I never in a million years would have picked Cassady out as a woman who spent her nights talking dirty on AOL. She was classy and cute, the kind of woman who could easily go from wearing a business suit at a board meeting to sporting a little tennis skirt at the country club. When we met for lunch at her hotel during her Vail business seminar, I was fully aware that normally she would not have looked twice at me in a hotel unless I was the guy bringing room service to her door. The magic of blue rooms.

I was nervous. She was not. This made me more nervous.

"OK, Flan," she said, touching my ponytail. "I like the way you look. A lot. Let's do it. My room, tonight."

"Doing it," in Cassady's case, meant things I couldn't quite imagine. She had wanted every detail of my teenage gay relationship with my best friend that lasted all the way through high school. She was way more interested in talking about it than I was. I never even talked about it with him back then—it just was, then we graduated, and it wasn't anymore.

"We were usually afraid of being discovered," I told her. "Mostly we sucked each others' cocks and gave hand jobs."

"Both cocks always at the same time?" she asked.

"Not always, but most of the time. We were teenagers. Who could wait his turn?"

It was harder to tell her the details about Bill, the love of my life at nineteen, the man with whom I discovered everything that mattered. The man who could sit and play Shostakovich so passionately that I was driven to fuck him right there on top of the piano.

When Cassady moved a little closer to me at our table at the Brasserie Z, grabbed my hand, and placed it directly on her crotch, I could feel the wetness through her tight jeans. I kissed her hard, right there between the cheesecake and the check. Hard and deep, the way men like to kiss, no soft, romantic girl stuff. It was the kind of kiss that you can feel right down to your cock, the kind of kiss that definitely wipes the lipstick right off of a woman's mouth.

"Ten o'clock, Flanagan," she whispered afterward, passing me a key. "I'll be ready for you."

I was hard the minute I walked in the door of Cassady's room that night and saw her dressed in a white button-down man's shirt and plaid boxers. She wore no makeup. It was cute, but it was damned sexy too. Her shirt wasn't buttoned, and I could clearly see the hard nipples on her flat chest. She had a tiny, angular body that was more little boy than grown woman.

She never said a word. We ripped each other's shirts off at once. In spite of being so much smaller than me, she was more physically aggressive than any man I'd ever known.

She got me on the bed and stripped the rest of my clothes off, until we were down to just our boxers. We wrestled for position, laughing, grunting, playing, kissing, her hands getting tangled in my long hair, my hands barely able to get a grip in her short blonde locks.

She climbed on my face and went down for my cock. Her pussy was in my mouth and she was riding my tongue and taking my cock in to the back of her throat at the same time. My hands were on her ass, slapping her bottom and spreading her cheeks and my fingers were starting to slide toward home. I knew what she wanted and I knew how to give it to her.

I rolled her off me, flipped her on her belly, wrapped my arm around her, and held her down hard. The power struggle is such a big part of it—who's fucking whom is always the question, and part of the fun and the passion. I spread her legs with my free hand and my knee while I oiled my cock, then positioned the tip at her ass and began the tease.

"Tell me you want it, baby," I said. "Tell me how bad you want it."

"Fuck me," she ordered in a voice as firm as any man's. "Fuck me hard." She moved her ass up to meet me and that was it; I had no more control. I was sliding into her hard and deep and there was no waiting and no feeling except pleasure and lust and that hard animal longing when nothing else exists in the world but your body and what it absolutely needs.

I came long and hard up inside of her and she reached down and touched her clit and came right after me. We didn't move for a long time; I just lay flat out on top of her and crushed her into the bed.

A half hour later we were up and energized, laughing and ready to go again. "Wait," Cassady said when I slid my fingers hard up inside of her. "I brought my cock, it's in my suitcase. It's my turn now."

We've finished dinner and Ruby sits and relaxes with Nita and watches me clean up, our standard deal.

"I think it speaks well of my life, Ruby, that I always do the dishes, and with a smile." OK, so I'm digging, but she brings that out in me, this need to be a little better and more productive in my wandering life than I am. It's probably due to all the little needlepoint sayings hanging around her kitchen, particularly the one I'm staring at over the sink that reads, "Do you think it a small thing, to know how to live?"

"So, Erick, what have you been dreaming about lately?" Ruby asks me, one of her nosy-yet-loving, "I'm going to figure you out if it kills me" kind of regular questions.

"Well, I've been having the weirdest dreams, Ruby. I'm working in Alfalfa's, stocking shelves, minding my own business, and when I look up the store is quite crowded with rows of gorgeous men and women. They're all laughing. They're all much taller than me. They all have their backs to me and they're all wearing labels, great big black and white labels, sort of like nutritional labels on canned food. I can't read them from where I am, but I know I should try."

"Interesting dream, Erick—are there more men than women?" This cracks me up. Some days I think Ruby quizzes me so much because, although she embraces alternative lifestyles and counts all possibilities among her friends—lesbian, gay, bisexual, pansexual, pomosexual, you name it—it just drives her crazy not to know whether to set me up with men or with women. When she asks me outright, I tell her the truth—I don't know. Today it seems to be women, yesterday it was men, tomorrow I might have to admit that all I really want is someone to love me.

"I think it was forty-two men and forty-two women exactly," I say with a laugh. "It's a weird dream, though, because nobody is reading anybody else's label. It's like I'm the only one who can see them. There's one tall redhead who keeps turning toward me and then away from me, kind of a tease, like maybe she's flashing me her label. I get closer and closer, and she speaks to me in French, and I can't understand a word beyond 'bonjour.' She looks like a stripper. You don't normally see a lot of French strippers in the Alfalfa's health food store in Boulder."

This isn't a real dream, just another story I'm making up to keep Ruby at bay for a while, though it's true that I check out all the women at the store and wonder if they're kinky and wish they had labels printed on their backs, not unlike AOL profiles. But this redhead I'm making up is Renee, my third blue room encounter—or Renee as I had thought she would be. Renee had described herself as a tall, busty redhead who looked much like a stripper, and she sent me a picture as proof. Her fantasy was to see how many times she could come in one weekend. I'd been fascinated by women's orgasms for some time, so I thought it would be one interesting and educational weekend.

Renee was a surprise. She showed up six inches shorter than the picture and at least that much wider. In fact, she admitted to me, the picture wasn't her at all, but she had wanted to impress me because I seemed so different from other guys.

I looked at her hard while she confessed what had become obvious anyway. Well, I thought, the busty part was certainly true. And she was a redhead. Not to mention extremely kind and funny and more than a little sex-crazed. She said she would understand if I wanted to pass on the weekend plans. I considered this, but it occurred to me that there wasn't much point to my explorations if I wasn't going to open my mind to new and unexpected things.

I went for it. It was amazing. We worked on her fantasy with my fingers, my cock, my tongue, my words. I talked dirty to her in English and she understood everything; she talked dirty to me in French and I understood nothing, but loved it. She might be the most sensual woman I've encountered to date. The count was twenty-three orgasms in forty-eight hours. All hers. I learned a lot about myself and about sex that weekend: about body types I'd never considered attractive before, and about what truly matters in a person when it comes to lust. I suppose it might even speak well of my life that we still exchange email and are friends today.

"So, what happens in the dream, Erick? Was her label written in French?" Nita asks.

"You'd think so, but it's a dream. Plain English. It said—To prepare: undress and lay out flat on the salad bar and spread open. Garnish with olives and artichoke hearts. Likes to be eaten slowly. Devour with enthusiasm . . .what could I do? I wasn't even hungry, you're never hungry in a dream. But she had this long red hair and an incredibly great ass, so . . ."

I always try to go far enough with my stories to embarrass Ruby and Nita, but I don't think it's possible. "I sure hope you have safe sex in your dreams, Erick, sweetie."

"Safe? We're not just talking safe, but sanitary here. First, I put on those little plastic gloves we keep for the deli workers, then I visited the giant condom machine that always shows up in my dreams just behind the yogurt stand."

"And then?" Ruby asks, laughing.

"Then I delivered. Long legs spread right around the tub of feta cheese; olives, black and green, ran right down her belly; artichoke hearts unfurled and wrapped around every place else. And then, I ate. I swear Ruby, it was almost as good as eating here at your house, but there sure were no leftovers. What do you suppose this all means?"

Ruby's still smiling. "Two things: one, food is very sexual, Erick. And, two, your as-yet-unused college degree in drama has not gone entirely to waste."

We sip coffee on the porch, and I check my watch. It's almost time.

"OK, maybe I've had one other dream, Ruby. I've been dreaming of a woman named Isis."

"Isis?" Ruby says. "The universal goddess. To lift the veil of Isis is to pierce the heart of a great mystery."

That might well be an understatement. When I met Isis in the *ZiplessFuck* blue room, she would tell me everything and anything soulful about herself, but nothing practical. Like her real name. She only told me that she's in her thirties and sometimes visits Colorado. But she was glad to tell me that she likes to run through sprinklers and spin in the rain; that she has done lots of rock climbing as I have; that she is a serious student of aikido; that she has a passion for vampires and dark sex and the hours just before dawn. And that she likes secrets, and strange men, and that she dreams that somehow sex is going to save her life.

"I want you to save me," she wrote. "I want to be taken. I want to forget where I am, who I am, and never even think about why."

"All dreams are mysteries to me, Ruby. And you know, I have to go. I have a date."

"A date? With whom?"

"Isis."

"Yeah, right."

I kiss Ruby and Nita goodbye and head for my car, heat rising in me just from having mentioned Isis' name. After months of hot and mysterious talk with Isis, she wrote, "Meet me in Denver. I visit there often."

"Me too," I told her, giving away no more than she did, never saying it was only a forty-five minute drive from my home.

She continued, "At the Oxford Hotel, Room 346, at midnight on June 21, the solstice. The door will be unlocked and I will be blindfolded."

"And kneeling by the door, waiting," I suggested, trying to get in the game.

"No," she said, "I'll be hidden. I like to hide."

As I drive toward the Oxford Hotel it occurs to me that this is probably not safe sex. But if I can climb sheer granite rock walls without worrying about my body, I can sure as hell drive to a hotel and meet a woman I've never spoken to on the phone. I'm ready for anything—Isis could be a man, or sixty years old, or—heaven help me—a teenager. No, wait, I doubt a teenager would have booked an expensive room at the Oxford. Maybe with a little luck she'll be exactly who she says she is.

I'm dressed in black jeans and a black shirt, with my hair pulled back in a black band. I even carry my bag of tricks in a small black bag, trying to live up to my *ZiplessFuck* room name of "Wizard," even though I know she won't be able to see me. Where does a person hide in a hotel room anyway?

Room 346 at the Oxford Hotel has a plaque on the door that reads "The Cherry Creek Suite." The door looks to be held open by a piece of cardboard slid in between the lock and the door. I look for a clue on the cardboard, but it says nothing. Suddenly I'm flashing on childhood games of hide and seek and how intense and erotic so many things are as kids. I push open the door and hear Miles Davis playing in the background. "Dark Magus" Miles. There are candles everywhere, and the light is flickering on the high pale walls, giving the room an eerie blue cast.

"Isis?" I say tentatively, locking the door behind me as I enter. No response.

I walk carefully through the living area, past the bar, into the bedroom. More candles, a big four-poster bed, but no blindfolded woman.

I walk toward the bathroom, past the Jacuzzi, and think that at least she's got good taste in rooms. If she's here. Maybe this is all a practical joke?

"Isis?" Maybe she wasn't kidding and she does like to hide. I look under the bed, behind the drapes, behind the sofa, in the bathtub. Nothing. But she has to be here—the candles look fresh, and the music coming from the boombox is on track three and somebody had to have started it.

Maybe she needs my words. "Isis, baby, I'm here. Come out." I check the front closet but it's empty.

The closet door in the bedroom is half open and it looks empty too, but I open it wide to try to see in the candlelight. Her clothes are hanging there—beautiful, elegant dresses, three of them, and a long black satin robe. I finger the sleek robe, and when I feel a hand hesitantly touch my ankle, it takes as much focus not to jump and scream as it does when hanging onto a rock ledge by my fingertips. I move the robe aside and kneel down. She is beautiful, and looks exactly as she had described herself. Curled up in a ball on the floor of the closet, she is wearing only a tiny black satin slip and a matching blindfold. Her lips are full and red, her black shoulder-length hair is straight and shiny, and that's all I can see.

"Isis." I pick her up, pull her out of the closet, and lead her near the bed. I stand in front of her and run my hands down over black satin, and I'm in awe. Her body is hard but curvy, with nice small breasts, full hips, and an ass that feels like she's surely done more rock-climbing than I have. This woman must be drop-dead gorgeous in the light. What is she doing here with me?

"Wizard?" she finally asks, and I laugh to think that anyone else could possibly have found her in the bottom of the closet.

"Yes. I'm here." I lift her hair and begin to kiss her neck hard, the way she told me she likes it. She stands perfectly still for me as I work my way around her, kissing and biting. I come back to her face, tilt it up toward me, and set to work on her lipstick. The blindfold is driving me crazy—it's very big and distorts her face and I'm craving the sight of her eyes.

"No," she says when I ask if she wants to take it off. "I never want to see you. That would ruin it."

She has an accent, a slight accent, but a familiar one. I can't quite put my finger on what it is, or where I've heard it before.

I will make this woman forget who she is and where she is and anything else but the feel of my teeth and my hands and my body on hers. But first, I've got to see her better.

I wrap my arms around her and walk her toward the mirrored wall of the room. There must be a dozen candles lit behind us, all across the back of the bar. I position her in front of me, facing the mirror, and kiss my way down to her calves, then back up to her shoulders. One more long biting kiss on the nape of her neck and she's shuddering and leaning back into me.

"You're so beautiful," I tell her, holding her head straight so I can see her in the mirror. "So are you," she says, and laughs.

She has a long, elegant neck, black arched eyebrows that rise above the blindfold when she laughs, and I can see that there's only one problem with this ultimate fantasy come true, and I don't know if it's a problem that I can deal with.

I know this woman.

I *know* this woman. I know her name. It's Nobeko. She knows Ruby and works with Ruby's friend Annie Braverman. I've seen her in Alfalfa's often. God, she *is* gorgeous. She's one of the ones I've lusted after and wished had a label on her back. But she's got a husband, a reputation, and a respectable life.

"Wizard?" she asks, reaching back for me as I stand in a stupor, no longer kissing her. "What's wrong?"

"Ah. I was just admiring all the candles you lit, Isis. That must have been quite a job." I'm stalling. I don't know if she knows much about me other than that I'm related to Ruby, but she would surely know me if she saw me. Can I do this? I don't recall her ever lusting after me before based on my looks. Mystery has its advantages.

"The candles are for you, Wizard."

She turns and reaches her arms up around my neck, fumbles for my lips, and kisses me until I begin to forget even my own name.

I take her black slip off, then every piece of my own clothing. I hold her arms above her head and continue with the biting and the kisses. I follow our script and then I toss the script from my head. I swear I've never been so hot for anyone before in my life.

I know what she wants sexually. It has to be the sexiest thing in the world, to know the truth about what someone wants, to know what they need, what they crave. She wants to be taken, she wants me to make her dizzy, she wants a man who can make her faint from sex.

I lay her down on the bed and I work on her body, part by part, sort of like a masseuse does, only with kisses. I could spend an hour on just one of her shapely calves.

She wants me to leave marks on her body. I don't want to because her skin is so lovely. Maybe that's exactly why she wants to be marked; maybe she's tired of being thought so lovely.

I brought all the sex toys I own in my black bag. She wants to try them all. This is a secret that women tell me all the time in blue rooms: men are too obsessed with their own cocks. Women want everything else. I haven't talked to a woman yet who doesn't laugh about the Viagra craze, or just shrug at the concept that what women are craving from men is more hard cocks. You don't make a woman faint from sex by straight-fucking for an hour or two with your erection, I've learned, you make her dizzy by pampering her, devouring her, listening to her, playing with her, inspecting and loving every inch of her body, laughing with her and then fucking her hard.

"Wizard," Isis says, as I move from her breasts down to her pussy, thinking about which of the dildos I brought is going to fit most perfectly there. "Wizard. You are everything I thought you would be."

I check her blindfold. I'm checking it often.

"And probably more."

It has taken several hours, but we're there, exactly where I want to be. She's sighing, moaning, writhing under my hands. The candles are burning down to nothing. There is no more music except for the sounds of Isis. She is so trusting and open to me that I can do anything I want with her. She's had orgasms from my fingers and from dildos, she's had me bite her until she begged me to stop, she's had both nipples painted with her red lipstick and then sucked and chewed slowly, just as I have done with her lips. She's been dizzy way more than once, but I told her it wasn't safe to actually faint—because I know that then I'd have to take the blindfold off.

I only want one thing from her now in return and it's almost old-fashioned. I want to see the beautiful Nobeko riding on top of me, facing me, my hands on her hips lifting her up and down, my cock sliding almost out of her and then driving back in. I prop my head up on the pillows so that I can see it all perfectly. I move her on top and she's almost limp like a rag doll, but she's smiling and spacy and I just want to freeze this moment forever.

"Put your hands on my chest," I tell her, and she does. She likes to be told what to do. "Kiss me."

I can't wait any longer. With Nobeko's tongue in my mouth and her hands on my chest and my cock deep inside of her, I come, and it brings tears to my eyes. I gently roll her off me, turn her sideways, tuck her back up against my chest, and hold her tight, checking her blindfold one last time.

I feel like Cinderella. I've got to be out of here by dawn, before she suddenly changes her mind and takes her blindfold off and sees me. I cannot afford to fall asleep. I hold Isis/Nobeko close and she falls asleep quickly in my arms. I lift her up and carry her over to the closet and lay her gently on the carpet where I first found her, covering her with her long robe. Maybe she'll think she just dreamed me, at least until she sees the marks and begins to feel her body.

I blow out all the candles, get dressed, pack my bag, and leave. To walk away from someone I crave in order to leave her privacy and respect intact, even though it makes me sad—I don't know, maybe some day this just might speak well of my life.

Oysters Among Us

"Kisses are a better fate than wisdom."

—e.e. cummings

"Get an ice cube, Annie," Sam orders me halfway through our long-distance telephone conversation. He's in luck, I have my ever-present glass of Diet Coke on my desk and there's fresh ice in it. Otherwise I'd have to unlock my door and leave my office, and somebody would be bound to want to talk to me and thus distract me from the deep sexual space Sam gets me in through his voice and his words.

"I have it, Sam."

"Lift your skirt, Annie."

To surprise, to excite, to believe in; these are the things a good lover must do. Sam knows. Some days I think Sam is the biggest surprise of my life, though I may just end up being the same to him.

"What are you wearing underneath your skirt, baby?"

I'm a grown woman, yet he can make me giggle like

52

a schoolgirl. I have a client coming in half an hour and he knows I'm dressed for work, but he's right, I'm never straight underneath. I lift my long black skirt.

"Red lace, Sam, darlin', only my short red lace slip. No stockings. My black lace-up espadrille sandals. Nothing else."

"Perfect. Put your feet up on your desk and spread your legs."

I always do exactly as Sam asks.

"Close your eyes, Annie. Now touch the ice gently to your pussy, yes, yes, now move it up to your clit and tell me what it feels like."

I have all of my curly black pussy hair waxed off for Sam, which makes me incredibly vulnerable to every sensation. The ice feels sharp. Cold. Intense. Fantastic. "Oh, Sam, it almost feels hot. Intense, too intense."

"Good," he says. "Now, slide the ice down and slip just the tip of it inside of you and hold it there."

I raise my skirt a little higher so I can see this. The ice cube starts to slide in so easily, wet on wet, and it's starting to melt from my heat and . . .

. . . a knock on my office door.

"Oh god, Sam, there's someone here." I pull the ice away and try to gather myself.

Nobeko, who works down the hall, is at the door asking to talk with me. I tell her I'll be right there.

"I wish I were rich," says Sam, "and then I'd hop in my Lear jet and be there tonight to finish you off right, Annie. As it is, I have to fly coach to Seattle on assignment. I'll call you later. I love you, baby."

We say our good-byes, I rearrange my skirt, plop the ice back in my Diet Coke and wonder why it's so hard to find enough time and space in my life for the things that matter, for magical sexual moments that may never come again. I think about Sam wishing he were rich. What's rich? I know a few things, and I know that real worth is only found in love and friends and laughter and the art of living for today. Being rich is not any better than having great sex, in my overheated opinion.

On the other hand, poverty sucks. It says so in every single edition that I own of the *Kama Sutra,* not far from the chapter on sucking cock. Poverty is an obstacle to great sex, to ethics, to virtue, and to having Big Fun, it says, sort of. "Morality is a luxury which poor people can rarely afford" is closer to what Vatsayana actually said, and if this guy could come up with sixty-four different combinations of oral sex, I'm pretty sure he knew the score on most everything else.

Nobeko wants me to come downstairs, where we're working on the remodeling plans for my secret dream of a sexual space, which we both think beats talking about work most any time.

"Annie," Nobeko says to me as we browse through one of my twelve translations of the *Kama Sutra,* "don't you think finishing this whole room the way you want will be too expensive?"

I look around at what used to be the huge, bare, white basement room of our offices and I laugh. "This kind of ugliness shouldn't have existed in our world, darlin'. Especially when there's a stairway up to the beautiful walled garden. Keep going—make it a pleasure room built to the letter of the *Kama Sutra.*"

I can't help it—I need to have a serious erotic space of my own, and I might as well make it a space I can open up to friends when I want to. Sort of my own little Sin Den right here in Boulder. There are sixty-four arts for living right and getting sensual described in the *Kama Sutra,* but none of them ever mention how to get away from your kids and your work in the first place. I need to find more big empty white spaces around the edges of my life in which to play and laugh and love and dance and focus on the things that matter. And, I swear I'm going to put a private line in this room and label it "for phone sex only."

People often think that the *Kama Sutra* is just about sexual positions, but it encompasses all the sensory pleasures of daily life—good food, silken clothes, perfumes, music, paintings, gardens. Somebody should revise it for the twenty-first-century—how to live a sensual life while staying right in the thick of everything that matters; how to make each day voluptuous from start to finish. Of course, we'd have to update instructions like Art #48—decorating chariots with flowers.

"I can't wait to start having parties here. And to find out what your idea of this 'Better Than Sex' party might be," Nobeko says.

I laugh. I've worked with Nobeko Graham at the East/West Boulder Health Center for three years now. She's a masseuse and a fourth-degree black belt in aikido, but a *wannabe* architect/designer. It seems that all the people I know over the age of thirty want to be something other than what they are. Even my tax-lawyer told me the other day that he wants to move to Hollywood and become an actor. Personally, I just want to memorize the eight ways to suck cock from the *Kama Sutra* and then try them out all night, slowly, on Sam. That's me, Annie Braverman, naturopath and mother, but *wannabe* casual courtesan.

Casual—The casual touch of fellatio is Method #1—Nimitta. Clasp the cock with one hand, bring the lips close, cover the end with your fingers collected together like the bud of a flower, press the sides of the cock with your lips. Casual is the touch on the tip of your tongue, but "casual" should not be a word anywhere near the tip of the tongue of the suckee.

"Flowers," Nobeko says. "A hundred fresh flowers for this room every week. I can't wait." Her face lights up at my go-ahead for her design, and I watch her finish sorting through the books to make sure she has noted every page about the pleasure room. Nobeko has shiny black shoulder-length hair that swings when she moves. I know she's desperately unhappy at home, tangled up with a husband and at least one lover. I can't seem to help, though I've tried. But the way she moves around the office inspired me to take up aikido with her. Nobeko's work uniform is black tights, brightly colored sports-bras that show her hard midriff, and Birkenstocks. I tried to copy this style once, but eventually went back to my own flowing skirts and long earrings.

The pleasure is so deep when you watch people move the way they're meant to, when they're involved in what's true to their soul, the things that are "true north" for them. Watching Nobeko move is like watching one of our three office cats—Bertha, Blue, and Zenrose. Cats live in the land of true north, always doing exactly what they want to, whether it's sleeping or prowling or lap-warming or nibbling.

Nibbling—Method #2 is Parshvsatodashta, which I'm glad I won't ever have to pronounce because my mouth will be full. Nibble the sides of the cock, with your teeth gently, then only your lips, then back to the teeth.

"I love the soft lighting you've put in here, Nobeko." I'm starting to picture myself nibbling on Sam right here in this room. "We need lots of candles too. And the brocade on these pillows is fabulous. Be sure to go to the Hangouts store on the Pearl Street Mall for those great swings. Songbirds and mynahs in wicker cages! I can't wait. Call China about bringing some of the garden inside." My friend China is an accountant, but a *wannabe* chef/gardener. I've been writing down erotic fantasies for her in exchange for her sharing her research on recipes for aphrodisiacs.

"It's going to be gorgeous," Nobeko says.

"Yes, yes. Just walking in this room is going to make anyone feel younger and more sensual. It will be better than sex itself. There will be no external pressures from the outside world in this room."

External pressure—Method#3—
Bahihsandamsha.Bring your lips close to the erect cock, press the mast and kiss it while sucking as though you were drawing it out and into you.

It's not exactly as though I don't know how to suck cock, it's just kind of the same theory as golf. You can play just fine, but once you get a pro to help fine-tune your swing, suddenly it's a whole new ball game.

Nobeko doesn't ask where the money for the room is coming from. Nobody ever does once I say I'll pay for something. They must just think my naturopath practice is real successful. I have two things I never discuss with anyone because it alters their perception of me permanently—my money, and my age. Not with friends, not with my kids, not even with Sam. "Age is just a number," I tease the kids. "I was born in the year of the Cat," I told some friends recently at a Chinese restaurant when the subject of birth-years came up, and even Sam, the smartest man I know, didn't blink. Or if he did, he looked away.

We're working on drawing the kinkier sexual positions from the Book and some of the sixty-four arts on the walls that are now sky blue. I want to be able to come in here for my rituals before I go to San Francisco to see Sam or before he comes here. When I go to see him, I like to work myself into a certain kind of sexual state, where for one week before, I never let myself come, never climax, just tease myself until I'm crazy mad for his touch.

The Tease—Method #4—Antahsandamsha. Let the cock penetrate further into your mouth and press it with your lips and then take it out. The *Kama Sutra* doesn't really call this the tease, but we sure used to call it that in high school.

I hated my family when I was in high school. My father was evil, my mother clueless. Then, as a complete surprise, I inherited money from my uncle who lived in Europe. A lot of it. Sixteen million dollars. But I hated the money. Back then I didn't grasp the theory of poverty sucking. Thank god I didn't just give it all away because I couldn't handle it. I spent a lot. I told everyone about my money, and I was used. People simply expected me to pay for everything. Being rich made me miserable and it sure wasn't better than sex. So at age twenty-two I changed my name, moved to Denver, and spent a few years as a sad poet girl/student wandering the bars of LoDo, fucking my brains out, looking for a place to belong as just myself. I sometimes used the money to help friends secretly, paying off their over-extended VISA's and investing in their businesses without telling them. But I've learned that it takes a lot more than money to make peoples' dreams come true.

So when Sam says he wishes he were rich, the guilt rides high. Will I ever tell him about the money? Should I? I think about it sometimes. I've thought about telling him in the middle of sex, you know, that moment when a man is under your complete control and you can tell him anything. Riding high on his cock, his hands hard on my hips, maybe just before the point of coming, I could say, "Oh by the way, I've known you for almost two years and we're so intimate and truthful and loving with each other, but there's this little thing I forgot to tell you—I'm pretty damned rich." Would he come, or would he wilt? If I ever admit my wealth, will it change the beautiful, erotic thing we have going? Will he stop trusting me? I circle round and round this question and can only come up with silence.

Encircling/kissing—Method #5—Cumbita. Encircle the cock with your hand instead of your lips for a moment, and kiss it as though you were kissing the lower lip of the mouth. Right side up or upside down, a passionate, sucking kiss here has been known to transform men's minds.

One day during my miserable young-rich years I went to Red Rocks Amphitheater at dawn and was transformed. I heard voices. I thought I could kiss the sky. I decided to accept and embrace my sexuality that is always on overdrive. I made a plan to do something useful with my life, and then went on to adopt my kids. I've figured out that money and energy underlie all of our dreams. But I'll be damned if my kids will know that they can afford anything they want at the mall, or can buy most of the stores in the mall, for that matter. I'll help make their dreams come true, but not that way.

So, can I pay for a pleasure room? No matter what it costs, it can't be more than a couple of weeks' interest income on my trust account.

Nobeko has finished browsing the books, and I write her the blank checks she needs to finish the room.

Browsing—Method #6—Parimrisktaka, or browsing. With the tip of the tongue, lick the mast all over and titillate the opening. Browse like he's a bestseller.

"I'm really sorry I missed that Skydancing class you guys went to," Nobeko says, closing the *Kama Sutra* and preparing her lists.

"Yeah, Sam changed a little at the Tantra class, all of us did. We decided we need more soul in our lives and more sex in our souls. We agreed we should eat more oysters and more chocolate, pour kindness down like honey, find sex in our laughter and laughter in our sex. We were at a pretty high altitude, but I swear, it all made sense."

"Yeah, most of my clients tell me that their sex life sucks. Not that I can speak." Nobeko shrugs. "They often say that my massage is the best touch they've had in years. It's kind of sad."

"Well, we're going to have parties here in this room, sweetie, and help liven everybody up. Let's do the 'Better Than Sex' party after I get back from San Francisco. What do you think?"

"I'll be there," she says. "I'll be the one hiding behind the mango tree." She laughs and leaves the room to me.

Sucking the mango—Method #7—Amrachushi-taka. Press hard on the half-entered cock and suck while pressing, using the base of the tongue, as when sucking the juice of a mango.

Oh man, I like this one—it makes me hungry just thinking about it. I stay in the half-finished room, lock the door, lay back on the pillows with my feet up on the baby blue wall and, touching myself, begin to see and taste visions of my favorite obsession.

I close my eyes and I see cocks. Nothing but cocks. A room full of them: big and small, hard and soft, circumcised and not. They're all gorgeous. I kneel in the middle of the room and they begin to talk to me in tongues. I recognize some words. I think they're being polite and telling me their names—*pinga! polla! minga! cu! der Schniedel!*—they say. None of them exactly have any faces attached, but they are all very friendly. There are pillows covered in purple and black brocade and cocks of every style recline on them, beckoning, calling to me, saying "touch me," "nibble me," "I'll take browsing," "suck my mango," "da mihi basium Anna"—and I swear that last one sounded just like Sam.

All these cocks are happy, man, I mean seriously happy just exactly as they are, and raring to go as we all should be. They know "true north"—in fact, I think they're all pointing there. Except maybe that one; he might just be thinking too much, a secret wannabe Latin scholar. I lift my skirt and begin to crawl around the room, and I know that if I can just go fast enough and try hard enough I can treat each one at least eight different ways. My mouth opens wider and wider, and I think maybe I can take them all in at once and I begin to try.

I'm wearing bright red lipstick and it leaves a perfect imprint on each and every cock in the room. The color is "Ramblin' Rose," I tell der Schneidel when he asks, and he approves and winks at me in that special way cocks have. Rings of red, kiss prints of red, great glorious smears of red up and down every mast. I like the way it looks so much that I stop browsing for a moment to pull the tube out of my tiny pocket and make my lips freshly red before I begin to devour the other side of the room . . .

> *Devouring*—the final method. Make him come, continuing to press it up to the end. Put the whole cock in your mouth and press it to the very end as if you were going to swallow it up.

. . .and the room is threatening to swallow me up and I love it. I devour everything in sight and each one begins to thank me—*merci, gracias, danke.* They say I've made their dreams come true . . . the one that says "tibi gratias" looks like he's going to follow me home, but I sneak out the door and hide behind the mango tree until they've all gone limp and curled up and fallen asleep and there is no more cockteasing to be had.

I think it's way past time to go see Sam.

The Church of John Coltrane is on Divisadero near the Haight in San Francisco. Sam and I go there to listen to the "service" of Coltrane's music when I arrive on the next Sunday. We hike the hill on California Street to the labyrinth at Grace Cathedral, quiet together. We light candles for each other and for our loved ones. Neither one of us believes in organized religion, though Sam struggles with his Jewish heritage all the time.

When we get back to his place in North Beach, Sam cooks for me, about the sexiest thing a man can do short of tying me to my four-poster bed and fucking me hard. Sam, my journalist/political analyst but *wannabe* novelist/playwright, is a great cook. An omelet with smoked oysters and jalapenos, sourdough toast, and fresh orange juice appear. I tell him about China's new fetish for cooking for sex, for finding out everything there is to know about foods that have been considered aphrodisiacs throughout history.

"I'll help her," Sam says with a laugh.

A pause. I can't remember feeling jealous about a man since I was a teenager, but I'll be damned if that isn't the feeling rising in me. Especially since I remember that China's been borrowing all my kinky leather-and-lace catalogs lately.

"Oh, I don't know, Sam, I think she's doing real well by herself, testing everything out on Jack. In fact, she's putting together a cookbook of sensual recipes, and she's going to try some out at our 'Better Than Sex' party on the sixteenth. People will have to either bring something or tell a good story about one thing they consider to be better than sex. Kind of like show and tell."

Sam hugs me close. "You know I can't be there on the sixteenth, Annie, but I'll send you as my one thing. You, Annie, aside from sex. Every time you come here you bring light into my life, and you're better than sex just sitting there."

I think that's cheating, but I love it. I put on some music, Van Morrison, and begin to dance for Sam while we talk. I know what he likes. Part of the joy in having a long-distance lover is in the wait, the preparation, the tease, the hundreds of hours spent thinking about him, the promise. I always go to the Montana Salon before I get to

Sam, and he doesn't even know all the effort I put into it. Seaweed wraps, waxings, temporary henna tattoos, black roses on my fingernails, always something new. It's Kama Sutra Art #58—the art of disguise. To surprise, to excite, to believe in—this is what I aim to do.

That, and to strip down to my new black lace bodystocking that makes me feel like a cat. I strip very slowly for Sam and climb up into his lap and begin to kiss him and stroke him through his jeans, casually, heading toward Method #1.

> *Sam Cooke is on the radio*
> *and the night is filled with space*
> *and your fingertips touch my face*
> *You're a friend of mine*
> *and I'm real real gone.*

He stands me up and places my bare feet on top of his and we begin to slowly dance. His hands, his big hands around my wrists blow all my method-plans away, and I am ready for anything he wants.

He holds my hands behind my back as we dance, taking control of every inch of my body that way, making me feel like a little girl. Sam is eight inches taller than I am and somehow this makes our bodies fit together perfectly, as though they were made from two halves of the same mold, bending and melding together at just the right points. His cock, his hard cock pressing up against my belly is as sexy as anything I've ever known—it's like being thirteen again and feeling a boy's hard-on desperately pressing into me through our clothes late at night at a junior high school sock-hop, when there surely must be three hundred and ninety-seven ways to say "I want you," but nobody—nobody—says a single word.

Sam knows exactly what to do. The standing positions,

the picture-positions they call them in the *Kama Sutra*—
the ones exalted in sculpture because they are so beautiful
and so intricate—these are what Sam likes best. He dances
me over to a bare wall and presses me up against it, running
one hand down over my hips to find the opening in my
bodysuit. His fingers, Sam's fingers, there should be three
hundred and ninety-seven names for Sam's long fingers and
what they can do to me as they reach up so easily inside of
me and begin to change the way that I breathe.

He finally drops his jeans and his boxers and begins to
lift me up, still pressed against the wall, my hands caught
behind me, his hands sinking into the black lace on my
ass, lifting me until I am just the right height for his cock.
He kisses me hard, sucking in my lower lip just as he slides
my pussy down onto the tip of his cock, holding me there,
kissing me, taking my breath away completely. My legs
wrap high and tight around his back and my hips begin to
move up and down as much as they can, begging for more,
finding more, taking him all the way up inside hard and
fast. He pounds up and into me against the wall, almost
cruelly, harder and harder, his tongue deep in my throat,
until I am coming for him and my heart is somewhere on
the ceiling and his hands have moved up to wrap into my
long hair and he comes for me and we collapse to the floor
and stay there for a very, very long time, until there is no
more music and a little more breath and nothing else exists
except for that sound.

We shop, we talk, we walk. Sam collects art like a
grown-up, and he's taught me a lot about it. When we're
talking about art collecting, it comes through quite clearly
just how much Sam hates rich people. I don't know if
he'd make any exceptions. Personally, I have no taste for
expensive things. Like a kid, I collect weird things—crystal

trains, black candles, antique white lace, leather bracelets, butterfly paraphernalia for my kids, erotic poetry—and I'm always on the lookout for new versions of the *Kama Sutra.*

On a warm sunny day strolling down Columbus Avenue, Sam talks about Rome, where he often says he wants to live. Holding tightly to his arm and still feeling that wall pressed against my back, I think about telling him that I could afford it if we wanted, but something stops me. I've learned not to undermine anyone's independence—mastering the art of living is something we all have to figure out how to do for ourselves. But if he just knew to ask me the right questions deep under the covers in the hours before dawn when his hard body is wrapped so tight around mine, I could surely change his life, and mine.

Now, you'd think that the *Kama Sutra* would have covered all the cocksucking positions . . .

As the days pass I tell Sam about my studies from the Book and we laugh and begin to practice positions Vatsayana forgot. The baseball position—I lie naked between his legs and pleasure him while he watches the Giants game on TV. The kneeling in church position—behind the screened walls in Grace Cathedral where this surely must be the best of sins. The tied to the bed position, where there's nothing to do but open my mouth and submit. One morning I show him the Altoids trick—suck the mint, peppermint flavor only, then suck the man—and he tells me it's as though his cock is tingling and on fire, in a good way, and we laugh so hard that I nearly choke on the third mint.

It's after the laughter that I start to tell him.

"I could buy a lot of these mints, Sam."

He just laughs. "I'm a forty-three-year-old guy, Annie.

You're killing me. We don't need too many more mints. We're just about right as we are."

"You don't want anything else?"

"Oh, Annie. The things I'm wanting in my life right now can't come from you.

Maybe it's true. We don't need much else beyond what we have.

I arrive back home, secrets still intact, and by Saturday we're ready for the "Better Than Sex" party. The basement pleasure room looks exactly as it did in my fantasy when all the cocks were visiting me, except that now there's food, and faces, and all the cocks are dressed in khakis and jeans.

The Book describes it so well:

> Let your house for seven days and nights be filled with singing, set musicians behind carved screens to play as you bathe together. Decorate with flowers and fragrant perfumes. In your garden, plant beds of green vegetables, bunches of sugar cane, clumps of fir tree, the mustard plant, the parsley plant, and the fennel plant. Clusters of wild jasmine and yellow amaranth, Arabian and Spanish jasmines, the frangipani. There should be a whirling swing and a common swing. Carry on amusing conversations on various subjects, and talk suggestively of things which would be considered coarse elsewhere. Sing, dance, play on musical instruments, talk about the arts, and persuade each other to drink.

Nobeko and China have finished the room off to perfection. Nobeko has even installed a special shelf for all my *Kama Sutras* and the rest of the sex books, while white Mexican church candles line the long high oak shelf on either side of the books. I notice China has shelved her *Joy of Cooking* right up there next to my *Joys of Fantasy.*

My phone has even been installed. It's fire engine red, and somebody's labeled it "the hot line."

Everybody comes to the party—who would miss a "Better Than Sex" party? Flanagan, my favorite hippie kid, is here; his cousin Ruby and her partner Nita; China and Jack, of course; Nobeko, by herself; Bill and Doug, who run the bookstore near the office and an underground 'zine; and about ten others. No Sam, he's in Boston. I know all these people well, but I realize they don't all know each other.

"What a gorgeous room, Annie," Nita says, "and the food!" Nita wears little gold snowflake earrings pierced in each of her ears, at least two, and sometimes more. Tonight there are three in one ear and four in the other, shining beneath her very short black hair. I realize that I've never even asked her why she wears them. It's funny how you can think you know your friends but forget to talk about the things that matter.

"The food is all courtesy of China," I tell her. "So are the plants, and the water garden in the corner. She's an artist."

China blushes, but she's a little devious beneath that innocent blush. She told me that every single dish she prepared is an aphrodisiac—there's saffron fettuccine with fresh lavender, white asparagus and crab meat salad, oysters Casino, a sauce of truffles, a chocolate rum trifle, and more.

"Sort of a group test," she said with a grin.

People are strolling around talking, just like a normal party. This will never do. The next thing you know I'll be hearing talk of real-estate prices or something.

I position myself in the high swing over by the two mynah birds, who never speak of money. In fact, they apparently don't say anything yet except "hello," but Flanagan, one of the freest souls I know, has promised me he'll teach them all the dirty words he knows and a couple more in French. Art #43—teaching parrots and mynah birds to talk. I asked Flan to also teach them to say "Hi baby," just like Sam does, so that I can melt a little each time I enter the room.

"OK, you guys, first I think we need a name for this room. 'The Pleasure Room' sounds a little, well, conservative to me, even if the *Kama Sutra* does call it that. They had these rooms all over back then, but I'm pretty sure this is the only one on Walnut Avenue here in the twenty-first century."

Lots of names are suggested, including my own: "The Sin Den," but we decide that the room should have a name you can say innocently in front of children. "I'm going over to the Sex Cellar, kids—be good," just wouldn't fly.

"I think with all these shades of blue and indigo and purple, there's only one good name," Flan offers. "The Blue Room."

Yes. We all agree. "The Blue Room" could be a bar, a restaurant, a room in the library, a guest room at the White House. Or an erotic space that can shift the state of your soul.

China's lover, Jack, begins to strum the guitar that he found behind the carved screens. Some people dance a little, some sit nearby and sing along, and everyone enjoys great quantities of China's buffet and the punch she's provided. I don't even ask what might be in it, but it tastes delicious.

Nobeko dims the lights so that there is only a soft glow and the light from the candles high on the wall. We're all drawn to sit in a sort of a semicircle near Jack: in the swings, on the pillows, on the Oriental carpeting.

"Better than sex?" Nobeko says softly to start us off, and she leans back on her pillow to listen. I can't help but notice that she's got her bare feet up in China's lap, and that China, lovely China of the long flowing red hair, is gently massaging her feet. Others follow their lead, and there's a lot of touching going on. I flash on junior high school, as I often do, and I think I may have been to this party before, the one where it turns into a toss-up between spin-the-bottle and passing cherries from mouth to mouth.

"I'll start, for Sam. He mailed his in." Very much to my regret—at this point in the party, I need to be touched. What the hell—I scoot over next to Bill and Doug. They have always been such kind friends to me, ever since Bill first came to me briefly as a client.

He puts his arm around me; he is the kind of guy who knows.

"Sam said that I, in person, was to represent his 'Better Than Sex' moment, but I suspect it's not fair to offer up a lover, since they are sex for us, in a way. So Sam also says that 'Better Than Sex' for him was being on the night flight from Tokyo to Hong Kong a couple of years ago. He grew up a poor kid in the Midwest, and as he likes to say, 'Once poor, never rich,' except that he says it in Yiddish, which sounds way better. But that one night, looking out the window over the Pacific, he thought that he was rich, that he had it made, that he had reached a point in life where he was valuable enough for someone to be flying him all over the world and treating him right."

Bill hugs me, though god knows it's not my story.

"If he can be that serious, so can I," Bill says. "Better than sex for me is being alive for the gift of each ordinary day. At this point in my life, that's all I ask. One more day with Doug, one more day with T-cells, one more sunrise. I never had any idea it was all so simple before."

This is getting sad, but his words ring so very true.

China gets up to serve more punch all around, and I see Flan move over and tease Nobeko about replacing China's feet with his for a rub. She agrees.

"The Internet," Flan offers, "because I've learned so many things there. But, I have a list of so many other things, too. On certain days that are just right: snowboarding, rock climbing, a picnic on top of Flagstaff Mountain, a certain French woman who comes into Alfafa's and asks about produce in a way that makes me hard."

A guy, a kid, but I adore him. "My first one would be just the act of keeping secrets," I say. "I learned to do it for my work, but it's an art, and it really started for me a long, long time ago. Mystery is sexy." It occurs to me that maybe this is just something I've taught myself to say.

Ruby, my dear therapist/friend, who may be the only non-wannabe-something-else in life that I know, must be taking this all in with a critical eye. She smiles and offers something entirely different. "A Tibetan head rub," she says. "It's very simple, but better than a drug if you do it right. Everybody borrow someone else's head."

Here we go now—show and tell time. I laugh but nobody else seems to. I borrow Jack's head. Jack's one strange cookie and I know a few secrets about him that I may have to share with China some day, but he does have great long hair.

"Lie back in his or her lap," Ruby instructs, and I'll be damned if we don't look like a little daisy chain of, well, head-rubbers. I've got Jack's head, he's got China's, she's got Flan's, Flan's got Nobeko's, and so on.

"All you do is scratch with your fingernails, in circles, in exactly the same spot, over and over and over again. Let's try it."

She shows us the exact spot on top of the head, and we

begin. This is a trip. After a couple of minutes of the music and the scratching and our silence, I know that this might be not only better than sex, but better even than wine to relax you. Oh, to surprise Sam with this. That's it—I will do this to him, and then I will tell him everything I know, and it will all be all right.

I love watching people get turned on. I must have been a peeping Tom in a past life—I could watch this forever. Flan has continued caressing Nobeko's head after everyone else has stopped, and her eyes are closed and she's loving it. Bill and Doug have stopped and are kissing, long and slow, and it's so damned sexy.

"Kissing," Jack says, standing up. "That's what works for me. China and Nobeko and I practiced for this."

Seems to me that kissing is part of sex, but I'm not about to stop any kissing demonstrations to get technical about 'better than sex.' This is why we built the Blue Room, this is why China cooked all the food, this is why we're here.

"It's Annie's fault," Jack says with a smile, "she has all these sexy books lying around."

So very many kisses: the nominal kiss, the vibrant kiss, the rubbing kiss, the equal kiss, the crosswise kiss, and more. China's kissing Nobeko, Jack's kissing them both, and when they get to the reverse kiss I don't know if I can stand it any more.

For the reverse kiss, Jack sits with both women on his lap, their backs to his chest. He turns their heads and kisses them from behind, sucking their lips passionately, one at a time, and then both together. Everyone is paying very close attention. They're sighing and kissing longer and harder, and then Jack starts the kissing competition.

First, it's who can kiss everybody, which is funny and damned sexy. When he moves on to who can kiss the longest, I mutter something and go off to change the music.

I feel like I might die thinking about Sam's missing kisses, and this takes me by surprise. I hide behind one of the mango trees for a few minutes and I watch. Everybody's off kissing in corners now, just kissing, and not necessarily in the combinations I would have expected. None of this may be what I expected, but it is intensely sensual. We could always blame it on the oysters or the punch or maybe, just maybe, this is exactly as it should be.

The phone rings, the hot line, and it's Sam in Boston.

I take him behind a screen and I tell him things in a whisper: how much I need to kiss him and teach him my new Tibetan secret, how much I need him to touch me, how wonderful all these people are, how very rich I feel tonight.

"Get an ice cube, baby. Then, we'll talk."

Tigers Above, Tigers Below

*T*he first time the coins start appearing in Nobeko's lap is during a landing at Denver International Airport. When she sees them she assumes they have somehow fallen from her purse, and she casually plucks them from the folds of her skirt and drops them in her big black bag. Fifty-one cents—one quarter, two dimes, one nickel and one penny, quickly deposited before deplaning to meet her husband Jeremy, who is waiting impatiently for her by the baggage claim.

"Jeremy!" she cries, feigning enthusiasm upon seeing him after her long weekend in San Francisco. "I've missed you!" Nowadays she only smiles slightly to herself whenever she says his name—they had once considered naming their youngest son Jeremy Junior until a friend told her that little kids named Jeremy got called "Germy" by other kids. Nobeko insisted that they name their son Stephen after her brother. She has struggled desperately not to think of her own husband as "Germy" ever since, particularly when he acts just like one of their three children in need of her caretaking, or when he simply forgets that she exists except around midnight when he wants a quick fuck, and then he has to struggle to even remember that she has some other name besides 'mom,' or 'hey.'

The second time the coins appear, Nobeko is in the bubble bath, dreaming of strange men and what they will do to her, touching the soft skin of her inner thigh, the thick curly black hairs floating just beneath her hand, and she feels a little light-headed when she notices two silver dollars resting on the arch of her foot that is posed next to the faucet. It occurs to her that these coins aren't even made anymore, and that she hasn't seen one since her father gave her one as a little girl. Afraid to move her foot in case they might disappear, she contemplates who the last adult was to have given her any kind of surprise gift, and can't remember. Maybe it was the surprise she had given herself, when she woke up one day ten years into her marriage to realize she couldn't stand her husband, had forgotten who it was she had meant to be when she grew up, and that she could have better sex by herself on her navy blue bathroom carpeting than with the warm-bodied man who waited in their king-size bed.

She leans forward to pluck the coins from her foot before she finally drains the water. Upon examination they appear to be ordinary silver dollars, minted in Denver in 1934. She tucks them away under one of her three diaphragms in a bottom drawer before toweling off and examining her so-called perfect body in the full-length mirror on the back of the bathroom door:

Inventory: I'll be forty next month and people keep saying I look thirty, as though it should matter. I think about sex every ten seconds during the day, but never about sex with Jeremy. I can't feel anything. Why can't I feel anything? I weigh exactly 116 pounds and have been 5'7" since I was fourteen years old and much chubbier. My body is as hard as a rock and every woman at the health club says, "You're so lucky—you can eat anything!" and they are clueless. I only have to be obsessive; I only have to make myself crazy with controlling my days and losing my nights.

Stop. Inventory: Black hair trimmed every eight weeks to perfect shoulder length; a dresser full of black tights and bright sports bras, fifteen of each, for comfortably leaning over clients while I massage the stress out of their bodies; three children safely in bed, three children who will be grown any minute now and leave me alone with a man I don't want to touch.

Stop. Touch your nipples, pinch them. Count: there are three safe spaces in my life—the bathroom with a locked door, every mother's safety net; the guest room closet behind the old skis and skates where all the ideas still live; and the back hill at Silo Park where I can sit on a blanket in the sun and safely cry.

Nobeko lifts one of the four red scarves that are draped artfully across the corner of the mirror and ties one around her eyes, expertly knotting it behind her head. Lying on the bathroom rug with her feet up on the wall, she begins to travel into her shadow life, a world full of masks and laughter and tall men and women who tell her what to do and strip away everything and take away her control and make her try new things. There is feeling, there is hope, there is passion, there is the woman who parades as Nobeko the good mother and wife during the day but becomes 'Isis' in the hours before dawn. Isis doesn't worry about sex every ten seconds because all she can do is feel strange hands reaching down inside her, turning her inside out, rearranging her skin as though it were a simple thing to notice that she was wearing it with the wrong-side out, like a child who has dressed backwards. Then there is nothing left to do but to feel every sensation in the universe flow down from her nipples to her pussy, to touch her clit at exactly the right moment, and let the orgasms flow.

Returning the scarf on the mirror with the others that she once asked Jeremy to tie her up with, Nobeko remembers his laughter, her embarrassment at her desires, and she checks to see if the silver dollars are still in the bottom drawer. Perhaps they are meant to be a kind of prepayment for performing a nice blow job on the man in the bedroom who will nag her if she doesn't. There are so many tasks in a woman's ordinary day; this one often reminds her of the tiresome repetitiveness of doing the laundry, except that it doesn't take nearly as long.

"Have you ever had anything magical happen to you, Annie?" Nobeko asks her friend at work the next morning.

Annie laughs. "Magic? Every day. My kids, Sam's love, good friends, work that I adore. Why?"

Nobeko shrugs. "I'm just curious. But I meant real magic—more like a rabbit appearing out of a hat, or coins showing up out of nowhere. Something bizarre, something completely inexplicable."

"Nope. I used to have a lover who was a magician, and he showed me all kinds of tricks they use. It's all fake. There's magic in the world, darlin', but none of it involves a wand or secret words. Are you OK? How's Jeremy?"

Nobeko smiles and turns to leave. "Oh, great! He got that promotion so he's been pretty busy . . . " Mostly he's busy counting his money and watching TV, but people hardly admit these things as hobbies to themselves, never mind to friends.

Nobeko enters her massage studio and prepares the space for the day—soft jazz on the CD player, low lights, fresh towels. Ten hanging plants watered, all thriving because of the misting spray that runs most of the night. A tiny cubicle separated by beads from the rest of the room houses her business records, some favorite books, her laptop computer. With a half hour left until her first client arrives, there is time to check her email, find out who is hot for her this morning, and pop into a chat room called *ZiplessFuck* to try and connect with some of the other lonely oversexed married people around the world.

Inventory: Count them. There are four men and one woman right now who have never even seen me who would meet me anywhere I want to have anonymous sex. The "babe masseuse" is how I think of myself before I log on —I heard a client call me that once when he was on the phone and it made me laugh. 'I am a babe masseuse, I am only doing this to save my life' is what I repeated to myself a hundred times when I was so scared before I met the first anonymous man called 'Wizard' in a dark hotel room and let him strip me down to nothing and turn me inside out. I stayed blindfolded and have never seen his face, but his words still reach me every single morning in my mailbox and I may have to see him again.

Count: three diaphragms, three lovers. I wrote their initials on the back of each case. It seems the polite thing to do. It's the only device I can use safely, according to my doctor, and after all, after fifteen years of marriage, how often can it be used. Germy just thinks I'm obsessively clean. He was supposed to get a vasectomy eight years ago after the last child but didn't. He doesn't know I've also learned how to put a condom on a man's hard cock using just my mouth; he'd probably laugh at that too. I read it in a book. I practiced on a zucchini, because I have to be good at everything I do: you just have to suck the condom in right and then take that one long stroke with your mouth all the way down the guy's cock and let it slide on tightly. Men seem to like this a lot.

Stop. Count: I'm thirty-nine years old, I bet I've had some kind of sex five thousand times. I was young, then I was married, and now suddenly I know what it's supposed to feel like. I must be a slow learner. Its importance is overrated, Jeremy says, just do it and don't worry about it —he read that the average man spends a total of sixteen minutes a year actually coming, actually in the state of orgasm, so how much can it all matter? It's just a release, he says, a natural function. If that's true, then why are millions of men obsessing over sex right here on my screen?

Stop. Log off. Back to real life. Five clients today; three men and two women to de-stress and send home happy; a fast half hour workout at lunch; two kids to be picked up at four o'clock; a quick dinner; a child's music recital; help with homework; dishes, laundry, twenty minutes sanctuary on the bathroom floor.

The human body is extraordinarily beautiful when stripped of all clothes and in a relaxed state, regardless of shape or size. Nobeko has strong hands and arms and pampers her clients with soft quilts and gentle talk. Her first appointment is with a new client, Erick Flanagan, a young rock-climber she has met through friends. Laying him out on his belly on her table with just a soft cloth over his ass, she begins to work on his neck and shoulders slowly. Suspecting he has a crush on her, she has to smile as she listens to him chat and try to make her laugh. She tries not to look too closely at her clients' bodies anymore, which makes it damned hard to be a masseuse, and tries to remember how it was before she entered her hopeless sexual head space where every man who is kind and attentive and shows a little skin looks highly fuckable. *What would he be like in bed, what would he be like in bed . . .*

Finishing with Flanagan's strong legs and ass and

sending him off, Nobeko retires to the back room to rest.

Stop. What is wrong with me, I get wet just touching these people. This is not professional. Log on for just five minutes, open up that dirty picture of the woman with two men fucking her, find a stranger to talk to, slide my hand down my tights just for release . . .

Ten minutes later when the buzzer rings for the next client, Nobeko jumps up out of her reverie, reaches for the off switch on the computer and pauses only for a moment to scoop up the large gold coin that has appeared just above the Escape key. Placing it down the front of her purple sports bra, she straightens her tights, her hair, her smile, and goes back to work.

On her day off, Nobeko checks out a stack of books from the library: two books on collecting coins, one book each on magic and rituals, Thoreau on peace and simplicity, and *The Good Luck Book*, which she finds while browsing for the others.

The gold coin is a five pound piece from Great Britain, minted in 1902 in Sydney, Australia and it is valuable. Nobeko places it back under the second diaphragm, cleans up the bathroom while she's at it, and returns to reading.

Henry David Thoreau's To-Do List:

1. Rise at sunrise
2. Take a bath in Walden Pond
3. Clean the cabin
4. Go off on an adventure

It seems a reasonable list, and not unlike her own days; but she wonders what he did for sex. Maybe that was included in the 'adventure.'

Dressing in jeans, black boots and a big red sweater to go to lunch with her therapist-friend Ruby, a therapist that Germy will not even consider going to because he says none of their problems are his, Nobeko pauses to follow the advice from her good-luck book and tucks one of the silver dollars in her left jeans pocket. Keep a silver coin in your left pocket for nine days, it says, and your fortunes in life will change.

"What do you do for adventure, Ruby?" Nobeko asks over chicken Caesar salad and raspberry iced tea.

"I eat cheesecake for dessert," Ruby answers, eyeing the table next to theirs. Ruby is soft and pink and lovely, just like her name. Nobeko has massaged her often and is always surprised how purely sensual her plump white skin appears when naked. "You need cheesecake too, sweetheart," Ruby adds. "You're too skinny."

Nobeko laughs, but she knows the truth. She can gain fifteen pounds and protect herself from the looks of strange men on the street. Men like her the way she is now. When her father told her at fourteen that she was too fat, she starved and learned to move into a different body type. She's tried different weights since then, gaining and losing weight with each baby, up twenty, down ten, up thirty, down thirty-five. Jeremy never noticed any of it. This is the good thing about husbands, this is the bad thing about husbands: they rarely see their wives.

Nobeko shares the cheesecake with Ruby, but knows she will work out exactly twenty-five minutes longer tonight to make up for it.

"Not to preach, Nobeko, but every day's an adventure for all of us. I get my 168 hours a week just like everybody else, and how I choose to spend it and make it matter is my adventure. How's everything with Jeremy?"

"Oh, great. He got that promotion so he's pretty busy . . .but, Ruby, don't you ever feel like you need something else, like there are so many things you forgot to do, like all the adventure in the world is right there outside your window if only you had the nerve to reach for it?"

Ruby takes the last bite of cheesecake and puts her hand over Nobeko's. "OK, you asked, sweetheart, you get one of my Zen stories . . ."

A woman is running away from some tigers. She runs and runs but the tigers are strong and fast and gaining on her. She comes to the edge of a cliff and there are vines going down the cliff, so she climbs down and holds on tight to them. She looks down and sees there are tigers below her also. Then she sees a mouse nibbling away at the vine that she is holding on to. She notices a beautiful clump of tiny red strawberries right next to the vine, growing out of the sparse grass. She looks up. She looks down. She looks at the mouse. Then she picks a strawberry and puts it in her mouth and enjoys it completely.

"Tigers above, tigers below, Nobeko. We're born, we die. Everything else is just, well . . . cheesecake."

They laugh, hug, go their separate ways. With two free hours left, Nobeko stops at Alfafa's Market to pick up groceries and buys a pint of strawberries. She sits on the lawn at Silo Park in the still autumn air, on the back hill where only a few men pass by and check her out. After eating a few strawberries and shedding a few tears, she stretches out, puts one hand in her left pocket, lies down under a willow tree and begins to enter her land of waking dreams . . .

There are many tigers in Malaysia, my mother's homeland. The three tigers I can see are black with silver markings. They are big, but they're smiling at me, almost laughing, and they have silver coins where their eyes should be. They sit at the bottom of a narrow wooden stairway and I stand paralyzed in my long flowing red dress at the top and I am too afraid to come down the steps and go past them. I climb a rope ladder into a tiny attic space and I curl up in the corner and cry. I have wished the most evil wish a woman can wish—I have wished, more than once, that my husband would not come home, that something terrible would happen to him. I always wished the same thing about my father after my mother died when I was nine, because I would rather have been an orphan than live in that big house alone with him. The wish didn't work on him, but maybe now the coins are a warning, an omen, a sign of evil impending.

I lift my long red dress in the corner of the attic, just up to my waist. I am bare underneath, I am fragile, my legs are too thin, I am not strong enough to walk away. The tigers are still out there. I can see them just the way I can see spiders in the corners even though they're not really visible. I just know they are there. I am trapped. I touch between my legs to feel safer, and when I do, tiny gold coins begin to spin in the distance, spinning as though they are hanging from a mobile in the opposite corner, beckoning, flickering in the faint light, then disappearing only to reappear every time my fingers return between my legs.

I keep my dress up and I begin to pass the time making a little building between my legs out of scraps of wood lying around me. It gets taller and taller and taller and I think if I work hard enough it will be big enough to crawl into. I make a little window for the coins to fly through in case they fall down. My building is frail like a house of cards, but it is not a house that tigers could live in.

When I finish, there is one tiger coming up the rope ladder—I can hear him—he is laughing. I think he is coming to help me, to take care of me. He saunters over to my corner and I smile and the coins in the distance begin to jangle together like a wind chime, as though a strong wind had just blown through the room. The tiger opens his mouth and he has no teeth. I reach my hand out to pet him. He pushes my hand away with his paw, sticks his tongue out, begins to lick his way up my leg, and I begin to scream.

Nobeko wakes up with a start and looks quickly around. Not a soul in sight. She notices there are tiny willow leaves all over her sweater, as though a big wind had blown through the park. She begins to stand and check her watch, pulling her left hand from her jeans pocket, only to find a dozen tiny gold coins wrapped tightly inside her fist with the silver dollar.

In her car driving to pick the kids up at school, Nobeko turns the oldies radio station up as loud as possible.

Stop. This has to stop. I will fuck my husband every single day for the next thirty days. I will not complain, I will not hide from him, he is a decent man in spite of his coldness. He is more like an uncle than a father to the kids, but he is still decent. This is my resolve. I am not crazy, I am not cruel, I will try this and see if it helps. There are no tigers, the coins are just some kind of a joke, the past is the past, I will make no more wishes, affairs are a bad idea, this has to stop.

The new gold coins are five soles pieces from Peru. Nobeko cleans out the bottom drawer of her jewelry box and moves all the coins there.

The resolve is simple: evenings include dinner, dishes, homework, reading, one half hour set aside at 10:30 to fuck, then she is free to sit on the porch with some coins in her hand and look at the moon, a trick advised in *The Good Luck Book* for bringing peace of mind. Up at sunrise: bathe in a tub that doesn't quite resemble Walden Pond, clean the 'cabin,' do not set off on any adventures wilder than eating cheesecake. No more orgasms on the bathroom floor; they can only come from sex with Jeremy.

Ten days into the new plan, with a smiling husband who thinks she's recovered from her need for romance and talk, Nobeko notices that no matter what she does, there are no orgasms. She fakes it and acts as if things will change. She fucks him on the dining room table when the kids are out, she gives him blow jobs in the hot tub, she takes him for a walk to Silo Park one night and lifts her skirt and bends over for him to fuck her right there. No orgasms, no feeling, no new coins.

Eighteen days into the plan, Nobeko wakes up and considers her options: stay in bed? have another child? join the Peace Corp? go shopping naked at the mall? go back to school? smile and make breakfast for the kids? go mad? She opts for breakfast and continues on.

On day twenty-two, the day after asking Jeremy once again to just play and tie her wrists to the bedposts and take longer and do something different, like maybe go down on her, and hearing "no" as an answer, Nobeko emails her original anonymous Net-lover, "Wizard," saying only "Help. Call me at 2 p.m., 782-0232."

Stop. Think. I am crazy. I just gave my home phone number to a man I had a brief affair with, if you can even call it that. But he writes me every morning, fills my mailbox with jokes and kindness and sex, and may just be saving my life.

At 1:50 Nobeko removes all of her clothes and sits with the cordless phone in the back closet of the guest bedroom, curled up on the big black pillow she keeps there for when she hides out. Stacked up all around her are her old design and drawing books, from many years ago when she dreamed of building tall strong buildings that would keep people safe. She brings the bottom drawer from her jewelry box in with her and begins to lay all of the shiny coins on her thigh, in a row from big to small, as she waits for the call.

"How are you, Isis?"

"Great."

"Are you? I've been worried about you. I haven't seen your words in a long time. Tell me, how are you, *really?*"

Nobeko can't remember anyone ever asking her that, not quite that way, can't remember anyone truly wanting to know. It is a deadly question, one that even friends who care tend to avoid. Tears begin to flow, the coins begin to shake on her leg, and she tells him everything.

"Where are the kids?" he asks. "What if Jeremy comes home now?"

The idea makes her smile. "The kids are at their aunt's for the weekend. If Jeremy came home, he'd probably think I was sitting here naked in the closet making calls for the PTA. I swear, I could be a heroin addict and he wouldn't notice as long as we didn't run out of milk." She touches herself at the sound of his laughter, the sound of his voice like a river of stars flowing down from one heart to another, reminding her of who she can be.

"Meet me, Isis. Today. No blindfold. Give me your address, I'll come pick you up."

Here it is right in front of me, waiting for my attention. This man touches my heart, my soul, my body. He makes me want to walk out of here stark naked to meet him. Here it is, waiting for me to step past the fear and move forward.

"God, yes. Three o'clock. Silo Park, on the back hill. I'll be wearing red."

The last time the coins appear, Nobeko is pulling on her favorite long red dress and beginning to brush her hair. Three small bronze coins lay shining on the back of her black hairbrush. She picks them up and arranges them on her husband's bed pillow. Nobeko walks down the stairs and straight out the door and begins to create her own luck.

A Banquet of Breasts

*T*here is no better fuck than a woman in a Halloween costume. I know this as surely as I know how to whisper the words "tantric sex" to make a woman swoon, and as surely as I know that lust is the opposite of death.

I had my eye on Marie Antoinette, or maybe Cleopatra, or maybe both deliciously together, until the Marquissa de Sade walked in with her whip and pulled my attention away. Four inch heels on silver boots that ride up her thighs, a black catsuit, black hair piled high on her head, a short black cape and a leather mask that hides her features, except for gorgeously plump red lips. Silver chains and handcuffs hang from her belt, while her leather whip occasionally whistles through the air, making people jump. I have no idea who she is, but with an ass and an attitude like that, I aim to find out.

Come to Annie Braverman's Halloween Masque, disguised as one of your favorite characters, the invitation read. "Jack," my girlfriend China said sweetly to me before she left for Philadelphia on her week-long business trip, "you should be Vincent Van Gogh or some other famous artist for the party. You could be just like him some day." China's a little starry-eyed sometimes, but I think she forgot to check out the rest of Van Gogh's story. My girlfriend thinks I'm a talented man. She tells me this way too often. It's a bitch to have someone believe in you so much when you don't believe in yourself anymore.

So I kissed her goodbye at the airport and then found myself a more appropriate costume, as Don Juan de . . . Boulderado. A cape, some boots, my long hair pulled back in a ponytail, black mask, tight pants padded in the crotch and a trusty sword. Throw in a little swashbuckling and I'm on the prowl for the night. Maybe I look more like Zorro than Don Juan, but it will do.

There must be over a hundred women here, most of whom I don't know. I love women. They love me. I just love too many of them too often, and some might say that makes me a womanizer, or a bit of a cad. But just beyond the edge of the new millennium, I'd prefer to think of myself as a polyamorist, or at least a polyeroticist. Many loves, much sex, but always with China as my primary partner and love. The spice on the side is just that. Now if I could only figure out how to explain this theory to China and see if she goes for it.

The Spice Girls are here, mini-skirted and cute, but they're not my type. I like 'em strong and smart. Bill and Hillary have arrived, and I notice that tonight she's smoking the cigar. A woman with definite possibilities. The abominable snowman stands in the doorway, fully-furred from head to toe, grunting rather than speaking. With that kind of power on display, I almost wish it was a woman underneath. Several devils roam the room, and Tinkerbell looks ready to fly.

Annie's outdone herself—the street in front of her office building is cordoned off with ropes, and hundred of tiny white and orange lights brighten the night. The party flows from the street through her big blue basement room and out back into the walled garden. There's a bit of a Mardi Gras feel afoot. Annie's one of those people who can put things together that other people can't. She's become a good friend, but right now she's a person who knows way too much about me. The night after she responded to my ad in the newspaper, we met for a quick drink and made a deal—her silence with China about my secret life in trade for my free services.

It wasn't exactly a personal ad, just my tiny back page classified in Westword for my sideline photography business. "X-Rated Photographer—in your home or my studio" is all that it says, along with my secret studio phone number. Well, that, and it said something about young pretty models being needed. But Annie was calling to get a hot picture taken of herself to send to her lover Sam in San Francisco. She used a fake name, and unfortunately I didn't recognize her voice until I'd hit on her, making a few suggestions as to how we could proceed and how I'd help to get her wet and make her nipples very hard for the photo shoot.

"Porn is the only kind of 'art' I make money from any more," I explained to her when I sheepishly met her afterwards. "And I don't want China to know that. She thinks I'm living off my graphic designs and still painting all the time." I knew the porn wasn't really Annie's concern, but I turned on my charm. "Deliberate lewdness, Annie, that's what Nabokov called it, and he said the urge for an artist to create pornography is like the verve of a fine poet in a wanton mood," I offered, appealing to her intellectual side. "Picasso kept pornographic notebooks that were made public after his death. Even Mark Twain wrote pornography!" This is all true, but I'm not sure she was buying any of it.

I haven't seen Annie much since then. Tonight I'll just avoid her—she's busy hosting and fiddle-dee-deeing as Scarlett O'Hara. My attention belongs now to the mysterious Cleopatra who is standing close and flirting with me, her breasts practically hanging out of her purple silken outfit and her eyes so heavily lined in black that she might as well be wearing a mask. There is a trellis in the back of the garden that provides a good hiding spot, and I think Cleopatra would look lovely on her knees there with one of my hands holding her black wig, the other down her wispy halter top as I teach her the secrets of a "tantric" blow job.

Some folks may say that a blow job is technically not "sex," but it sure does feel like it in action. One thing you learn in the land of tantra is that most everything between two people can be a kind of sex. Hidden behind the garden trellis, I slide my cock from it's bulge, begin to part Cleopatra's waiting lips, and tell her it's all about breath control and opening her mouth very, very wide. She does this quite eagerly, and with my one hand on her nipple, pinching, I can feel her moving into the flow.

But the night is young. If I hold Cleopatra just to the right behind the trellis and close her painted eyelids with my fingers, I can watch some of the other characters pass through the garden and begin to contemplate selecting my second course from the dazzling menu that women so decorously display with their bountiful bodies, their alluring asses, their beautiful banquet of breasts. I am, as always, a starving man.

Cleopatra is grabbing my ass and going for my climax, and I teach her how to stop at just the right moment, lifting her up to me, kissing her hard, holding her tight, thanking her for her existence, letting my hard-on subside and my climax wait. I'm sure I'm not the only man around to know this secret of not coming, but women find it extraordinarily enticing. It never gets you in trouble. I have to save my energies, sampling each dish as it is served, never gorging too much on one course. Gluttony is a sin, after all, and the only sin I willingly trespass is the one involving lust. I lust in my heart, in my mind, in my groin, in my knees, in the bookstore, in my dreams, and most any moment of any given day when I'm avoiding my art and some luscious female form happens to pass through my vision.

So many women, so much time.

I always give them my card afterward, and sometimes they call later. Modeling is attractive to women of all ages, no matter what they actually look like. I'm not one of those guys who promises to make a girl a star, but I do promise to make them sexy, and I succeed, at least on film. I know how to turn women on, and a lustful woman is always attractive for that moment.

The X-rated Web site I shoot new models for wants mostly penetration shots with pretty young girls, but the variety of things that individuals want me to photograph are remarkable—toys, fingers, feet, spankings, latex, even butterflies. Some of those photos stay private, but some can be seen on the Internet on any given day—both on sleazy sites like alt.sex.anal and on elegant web pages. Women, men, straight, bi, gay, groups—I've done them all. No animals or children, though, I do have some standards. Standards, and lots of lubricant, since people tend to forget how nervous they can get before a camera.

This may not be real art, but it's fun in a dirty kind of way. "Nice" is always the enemy of art. I've been known to loan my cock for a picture on more than one occasion, since I'm usually hard once they get naked. The strangest kink-shoot so far was the woman from Australia who wanted to use her gravity boots and do everything upside down. Her name was Celia. She wore her blonde hair in pigtails and kept her short plaid skirt on while she removed her blouse. I keep costumes and props around to help out, but this gal brought all her own, plus a boyfriend.

"Jack," she said to me, "once I'm upside down I want you to do whatever I ask of you."

I did. The guy was up on a ladder, following her other

instructions and putting his fingers inside of her. Her little skirt hung upside down and her pigtails almost touched the floor. I put clothespins on her nipples while she moaned, and I got just the right shot of them hanging down toward her chin. She wanted her face clearly shown in every shot —normally I advise that people don't do this because they might regret it later, and I always propose the mystery of masks and wigs, but she was adamant. I put the leopard-print handcuffs around her wrists and the cigar in her mouth and took a whole roll of film. She had to have the cigar in her pussy next—everybody wants that lately— but this girl wanted it lit while the unlit end entered her. I let the boyfriend spread her legs a little wider and do the honors, but we both watched that cigar burn down while I slowly changed my film.

The final shot was her personal fantasy. Some people dream of white-picket fences; this girl wanted two men to fuck her mouth while she was upside down. The boyfriend started, I set up the shot, and then I helped. Two men kneeling, blond pigtails, a wide open mouth, two cocks forcing their way into her mouth at the same time—I've seen this posted on her Web page and elsewhere. My own face never ever shows in these pictures, but my cock is having its fifteen minutes of fame.

Marie Antoinette and Anne Boleyn are both flirting with me around the dessert tables out in front by the orange lights. I sure wouldn't mind being locked away in the Tower of London with this Anne for a thousand days, though as I recall, the King had her put there under the charge of polyamory. You could get beheaded for it in those days, now you can just get impeached.

The elaborate spread of pies and cakes and petit fours doesn't interest me—I'm more interested in a little pussy al dente. Or a lot of it—preferably two at the same time, since I notice the queens are flirting with each other. Anne is tiny and lithe and I'm trying to think of a graceful way to suggest that we sneak inside and up to one of the massage studios in the building, and that I lay her out naked on top of the taller Queen Marie with the perfectly plump hips and eat them both out together while they kiss. Sort of a stylistic tantric-torte, I tell them, a great delicacy in the *Kama Sutra*.

Either they believe this nonsense or maybe they're starving too, because the three of us wander away and upstairs without much more discussion. I help them out of their big skirts and petticoats, leaving their corsets and masks on for a little glamour. Marie Antoinette lies down on the massage table on her back and pulls Anne Boleyn on top of her, breastwires to breastwires. They begin to French kiss, and I'd kill to have my camera here for this pose, because there's some serious passion building. But there's work to be done. With my hands on the top layer of ass, I dive into the bottom layer of the Queen-torte, nipping and licking and sucking on Marie's pussy until she remembers I'm there.

Womens' pussies are the eighth wonder of the world. When I was a child I used to sit under the kitchen table all the time and look up the skirt of anyone who sat down. Other times, my older sister would sit at her dressing table and I'd hide underneath the bed and watch her tentatively touch her pussy as she prepared for a date. Women are so beautiful—I think maybe I was one in a previous life, or maybe I was just a pussy. If I was, I'm sure I was the shy graceful type, lips barely showing, clit slightly hooded as if coyly hiding, hair around me carefully shaved off to show my blush. If I was a woman today, I'd surely be a lesbian, because who would ever choose the ordinary roughness of my body over soft skin and curves and breasts of every size and shape and pussies, my god, pussies? Cocks can be bought in any shape or size, but pussies, pussies are priceless.

After Queen Marie comes for me, I turn them both around so that they're side by side and I can intertwine their legs and dive in and reach them both. My tongue and my fingers are fast and then slow, reaching, stroking, teasing, promising, delivering. Their clits taste like honey, and when Queen Anne moves her long lacy legs and wraps them so tightly around my neck, it feels like my head is going to come off. Queen Marie reaches down for my bulge, but I stop her and spread them both open together and take quick fast licks from one clit to another until they are both coming at the same time, shaking the massage table.

When we all recover, they help each other dress while I watch with fascination. Marie Antoinette poufs her wig and powders her face and pats me fondly on the behind before leading me back outside. "My dear Don Juan," she says, "let's go eat cake."

"Fiddle-dee-dee," I hear Annie/Scarlett saying with her charming laughter, talking to a group not far from the buffet tables. I bolt when she moves toward me so that I can avoid her, and end up down in the basement, where Hillary is talking with the Marquissa de Sade and a cool local minister named Jerry who I actually know. He is dressed up as Cary Grant.

"In my day, my dear," Cary is saying to the Marquissa as she twirls her whip, threatening every man in sight, "when we felt that way we just went and watched a violent movie."

The Marquissa lets out a decadent laugh. "In your day, dear man, evil was highly underrated."

Her French accent is fake, but her meaning is clear. My

kind of girl, no doubt about it. I ask her if I can talk with her a minute, and when we step aside behind a Japanese screen I say, "I am a starving man and you are the feast of reason that flows through my soul. I would be honored to sup at your toes."

She looks me up and down—taking in my fake bulge, my cheap mask, my boots that could use a polish—and she runs the whip over my cock and laughs.

I consider. If not poetry, maybe an offer of tantric submission for a dominatrix? Or a line suggesting she model her leathers for me?

She grabs my ponytail and pushes me down to my knees. "Do not speak again unless you can improve upon the silence."

I kneel; I obey; I wait.

"I've seen you around," she says. "You are a boy in need of better behavior."

I say nothing. It would be tough to disagree.

"Kiss my feet."

I kiss the silver toes of her boots like there is no tomorrow. She cuffs my hands behind my back; I crave only to touch her body once.

She examines me. Her gloved hands explore my mouth, her fingers silence my lips every time I try to speak my usual smooth words. She removes the stuffing from my crotch and tells me I don't need it, that all I am to be for her is my natural self, bare and always open.

She takes off my mask and she kisses me, her tongue driving hard through those plump red lips into my throat while her hand reaches down into my pants and strokes my cock. Maybe this is what I have always been waiting for. A woman who can take control of me, a woman who can let me soar like a kite and then bring me back down hard under control and make me do the things I am meant to do. A woman who can wrap her whip around my cock and balls and tease me into oblivion.

"You will meet me," she finally orders, "once a week. Wednesdays at 3 p.m. sharp in your studio. My name is Madelaine Penafiel; you will call me Mistress Madelaine. You will be silent, gagged if must be, and we will explore. It will be your services for mine. I can make you a better boy than you are."

She removes the handcuffs and the whip, turns on her silver heel, and disappears.

I am a changed man. I take some time to recoup and restuff and stagger out of the basement looking for her, planning to follow her home or maybe to the ends of the earth. She is nowhere to be found, almost as though she is gone with the wind, or perhaps she's behind another screen with another man. The party is still going strong, and everyone still looks the same, except for me. Scarlett O'Hara flounces over in her fluffy green dress with the tiny waist and asks me if I'm okay.

"You look upset, Jack," she says. "Did you talk with China?"

China? I am snapped back to reality. "No, why?"

"Oh, I tried to tell you earlier but you ran off—she's been here all night, waiting to see if you'd recognize her."

A sweat begins on my brow. "Which one is she, Annie?"

Scarlett looks me in the eyes and smiles slyly. "Gosh, Jack, I'm just a sweet southern belle, I don't know, it's so hard to remember these things." She arches her eyebrow. "Maybe I'll be able to think about it . . . tomorrow."

I consider that death might in fact be the opposite of lust and, with eyes wide open, begin to prowl the party one last time.

Naked at The Mall

I have twenty-four body piercings and none of them show when I'm dressed. With the five tiny holes in each of my earlobes, I'm up to thirty-four total. I have only one tattoo—my name, Nita de LosReyes, and my lover's name, Ruby Blackwell, are entwined in red and black around a rose on my ass. I am looking for the right spot to place one more piercing for my thirty-fifth birthday. I think it's all intensely erotic and that each piercing maps my personal expedition out of the underground life of a fact-loving fanatic married to a man I liked only as a pal, into a full-blown life of bliss as the partner of a New-Age, rune-reading, astrology-believing, pagan mystic lesbian therapist. My partner Ruby just thinks that maybe I was a human pincushion in a previous life.

"Get your tongue pierced, Nita sweetheart, and I'll never kiss you again," Ruby has threatened me more than once. I told her that her cunt would disagree and would love the feel of my pierced-tongue, but the truth is that I could never live without Ruby's long slow kisses, so I don't even consider going through with it.

My birthday falls on the winter solstice, the shortest, darkest day of the year. We celebrate the solstice eve with candles and bells and natural presents and all of Ruby's rituals. I've been sent to Alfalfa's to finish buying their entire stock of the little raspberry candles that change the aroma of the entire house. We will start the celebration at a Silo Park concert of "polyethnic Cajun slamgrass" music from the group Leftover Salmon, complete with bonfire, and then go back to our house to eat and put all the kids to bed and stay up to greet the dawn with a few friends in front of the fireplace.

Annie Braverman and her lover Sam will celebrate with us, as will Ruby's friend Madelaine, who runs some kind of motivational business and splits her time between Colorado and LA. She lives, when she's here, with two guys, who I know are both her lovers and her roommates—I just can never figure out who fucks whom and in which way, not that it's any of my business. I think she has at least a couple of guys living with her in LA too. Madelaine is tall and thin and has short cropped black hair like mine, but she is always surrounded by interesting, sexy-looking men. At least she's got the harem idea down right—everyone knows that a woman needs multiple men and not vice versa.

With twenty raspberry candles and the few last-minute items on Ruby's grocery list in my basket, I chat with Ruby's cousin Erick Flanagan who is working the checkout. He tells me he has big plans for his own solstice celebration. He's in love, he tells me: with an older woman, he says, looking at me as though I should understand everything this implies since I am all of eight years older than him, and they will be spending the night hiding out together at the Oxford Hotel in Denver. The sappy look on the face of this sweet guy in love might be better than sex, or maybe even tongue-piercings.

Walking the twenty minutes home to Ruby through the slightly chilly streets of Boulder, I remember how I used to celebrate my birthdays by running marathons. I only did a few things well, so I did them all the time: I was a Jeopardy almost-champion in college so I continued to study facts as though they mattered; I was born with a body meant to run, so I ran as fast as I could every chance I got; as a child, I learned to navigate the world by searching the living-room globe for my missing mother, so I grew up to be a cartographer who clearly defines the route home for other people. This is all I can do, I told Ruby when we first got together, these are the things I am meant to do. No, baby, she would tell me, and still tells me most every day, you only have to dream yourself into your reality—you can dream and visualize yourself into doing anything in this world you want to do.

Before Ruby came into my life, the only thing I ever visualized was naked people. When I was celibate for two years, I got through my days by thinking analytically: what's the big deal about naked bodies and touching and all the messiness of sex? Sometimes I would watch someone ahead of me in a race and mentally strip them—then I would know that they were nobody, just another naked body that I could easily pass by, and I would. I never even touched my own body sexually for two years, never had an orgasm. I thought of my body as an athletic machine, and I went to work on time every day and became an expert at mapping out the high country of the Rocky Mountains. Then Ruby touched me: without permission, without my planning it all out, with no map defining the way, and I began to melt like a simple snowflake at the first warmth of spring.

Ruby's friend Madelaine does some body piercings on the side, and I thought of having her do my birthday piercing at the bonfire at Silo Park since the weather's been so nice, but most people don't exactly get off on this like I do. Except for the teenagers, who think it's all "way cool." Ruby's fourteen-year old daughter, Cara, whom I spend half my life ferrying around town, looks at some of my more visible piercings with envy whenever we are naked at the health club. She tells me I should name them, kind of like pets, she says, or stars. The little row of diamond circles that run from my navel down toward my crotch should be a constellation, perhaps, a series of stars that light the way. I laughed when she told me this idea, told her that I refused to be the Big Dipper, and pointed out that unfortunately her creativity wasn't going to help her get her mom's permission for her own piercings any time soon.

"But, Nita, I dream my own piercings all the time," Cara said, "just like my mom always says to dream things you want. In my dreams I am the first fourteen-year-old rock-star-princess, and I have a tiara and everything. I have little silver rings in my eyebrow, my nose, and my lip, and I sing standing on top of a big black piano that has diamonds that light up all around its edges. I'm kind of a cross between Sarah McLachlan and Princess Di, only really young, and there are whole festivals built around me, and people worship me. What do you suppose this all *means?*" she asked me in the special I-want-it-now whine of teenage girls everywhere.

I am not a good mother figure. I should have told her all about waiting until you're older and can know what you really want, some wise words that would make Ruby proud of me. Instead I said, "Got me, Cara. Maybe you just need to dream it again and give your piercings names. I'm too old to do something like that, but you're not. My piercings just are what they are; silver and gold and tiny diamonds and rubies that mean a lot to me, but they're not like pets. Yours could be."

We laughed, we dressed, we went home. And then I began to name mine anyway.

"Cassini's Division" was the answer to one of the questions I did get right in the final round of college championship Jeopardy so many years ago. I can remember all of the questions, except for the final one that I blew, which was about love—a foreign subject to me at that time, no matter how much I studied. "What is the name for the black spaces between the rings of Saturn?" was the question I got right.

Cassini's Division—this is now the name for the diamond and silver rings that run from my navel toward my cunt. Even Ruby likes these piercings—she teases them with her tongue on her way down to my clit, she counts them slowly, she helps me take them out and put them back in on race days. She thinks we should replace the diamonds with rubies. But I got them exactly as they are not long after I spent that first night with Ruby in a remote cabin in the high country, caught in a snowstorm, discovering that I could not only love and even lust like other people could, but that I was capable of loving a woman in the way I had always thought I was supposed to love a man.

"Travel with me, Nita sweetheart," Ruby whispers to me now late at night as she starts in on my body with her oils and her caresses. "You still haven't been to so many places I want you to go." I am the strong one, yet Ruby ties my hands and ankles to the bedposts with her red scarves to keep me from trying to be in control. Her hands are so soft, so kind, so slow in just that right way that makes me begin to slip away from who I am and where I am and slide closer and closer to her enormous heart until I am enveloped in her warmth and there is no dark space at all left between her silky skin and my hard muscles. "Open for me, sweetheart, that's it, open all of the way," she whispers as her fingers slip inside of me, first one and then two and then more, until her entire curved hand is stroking in and out of my cunt and I know that I am dripping wet, but it feels like there is a waterfall that is flowing down over us and that if I open wider and wider and imagine that a million rainbow-colored rivulets of water flow inside of me they will do exactly that, and then Ruby slides her fist all the way up inside of me and I am home.

The solstice ritual is a primal experience, as almost anything done by candlelight is. So is running a marathon, a great concert, dinner with good conversation, or sex, if you're doing it right. If you can turn something "off," someone wise once said, it's not primal. And primal experiences are what everybody craves at the start of this century—experiences that matter. I gave up many things when I moved in with Ruby years ago—no more television, no daily newspapers to feed the disquiet of my mind, and as little excess consumerism as possible. Instead, I've learned to know when sunrise and sunset are and to observe them in silence whenever possible, to meditate, to garden, to eat natural foods, to take long walks with the kids and listen to them laugh, to have lots of great sex, and to find some peace of mind.

Unfortunately, with kids around, I can't give up all of the things that most people are amusing themselves to death with, like the teenage passions for rap music and Nintendo or the dreaded teenage trips to the mall. The harshness of spending more than ten minutes inside a crass, noisy mall crawling with holiday VISA-shoppers has begun to permeate my otherwise sensual dreams. But Ruby is teaching me to how to create "lucid dreams," dreams that you can control from the start. It's like visualization, except you're asleep. You wake up, you write the dream down, then you try again the next night to go where you want to go. I laughed when she first started teaching me this, then

I began trying to get past my block and dream toward my big goal of finishing my first triathlon.

I can run. I can bike. I can swim in the pool or occasionally in the Boulder Reservoir, but not in the ocean. I am strong, and although it's true that I could barely swim until I met Ruby and she made me work at it, I am a good swimmer and could do the required miles if it wasn't for the memory of my mother. My mother left home, disappeared on purpose, when I was a baby. When I was twelve years old, I learned that she had died in a boating accident in the Atlantic Ocean off of Brazil three years earlier, yet nobody had bothered to notify me or my father until then. Every time I get in the ocean water I see her: I see her face from the one young picture I had of her, see her struggling, see her unhappiness, see her giving up, and see her going under.

So I dream and I dream, and I train and I train. Every night, while I dream, Ruby holds me tight: she strokes my body, she kisses my neck, she loves me. She went with me to the first triathlon I tried in Santa Cruz and held me tight that night after I freaked out in the swim race, telling me over and over, "You don't ever have to do a triathlon, Nita baby, you don't have to do it." But we both know that I do.

I fall asleep trying to dream of myself in my black tank suit running out of the ocean and across the line to head for my bike, but I'll be damned if every time I mentally strip down all the officials and the other contestants and start seeing naked people, I don't end up someplace other than the race.

The first time I find myself naked at the mall, nobody seems to notice. I stroll in the north entrance by the food court wearing nothing but my Birkenstocks, with most of my twenty-four piercings shining under the artificial Christmas lights, yet not a single head turns. I walk alone toward the up escalator, and I notice that the entire mall has been painted varying shades of blue—navy, azure, indigo, lobelia, gentian, aqua—and that even the big central fountain is spouting baby blue water.

I am only at the mall to pick up one thing, so I stop in the music store first to buy the new KBCO Studio benefit CD release. "Nice outfit," a tall man says to me as I stop in front of the rhythm & blues display. He reaches over to stroke the three silver rings in my left nipple, stroking them the way you might pat a pretty velvet shirt someone was wearing when you complimented them. "Thank you," I mumble, feeling aroused at his touch while my nipple gets quite hard. "Aren't you Madelaine's new . . . um, boyfriend, Tanner?"

"I am," he says, continuing to run his fingers over my left nipple and then reaching for the other with his right hand. "But not a boyfriend exactly," he says with a grand smile, "I'm her slave."

He is fully dressed in normal clothes—wool pants and a button-down striped shirt—but I notice that he has a red leather collar around his thick neck, rather an ordinary-looking dog collar.

"Oh, I see," I say, standing very still while he pinches my nipples. "Sort of like a pet?"

"Yes, exactly. I go to my law office every day like a normal man, but when I come home I follow Madelaine's rules. I come in the door, strip off all of my clothes, put on my collar, and kneel naked in front of the fireplace."

"Oh, of course," I say, glad that his hands are so strong. "These are my stars," I tell him, nodding toward my nipples. "The left one is called Terebellum and the right is Cassiopeia."

"Would you like to have sushi with me?" Tanner asks, letting go of my nipples and paying for his four CDs. I nod, and we begin to walk the length of the blue mall, with Tanner trying to guess the names of the rest of my piercings. "Maybe it's the Big Dipper around your belly button?"

"No, no, that would be Electra. Names matter. I'm a map maker, and everything has to be perfect. There is a North Star, however, but you can't see it."

"I see. Well, I call Madelaine 'Darkstar' at home," he tells me as we enter the Four Happiness restaurant and take a seat at the bar, "and as soon as I come home from work she gives me directions. If she's not there, she has my evening mapped out for me on 3 by 5 cards. Sometimes she merely leaves her black leather riding crop out in my spot by the fireplace and then I know I am to come to her bedroom and serve her."

There is a big turquoise serving table in the window of the restaurant and vases of blue roses everywhere I look. The sushi chef walks over toward me, looking angry. "We need your body as a platter," he yells.

They lift me up and lay my body across the big turquoise table and begin to shake all of the roses above me to let the petals fall where they may. Tanner takes my sandals off, lifts my arms above my head, and holds me very still until there are a thousand blue rose petals covering my body. It is almost like being dressed.

"Chopsticks only," the chef instructs the patrons as they gather around. "You may not disturb the rose petals." He arranges all of the sushi elements down my body on top of the rose petals—tuna on Terebellum, octopus on Orion, eel on Electra—and everyone begins to eat.

I definitely write that dream down.

One of the problems with having a therapist for a lover is that they make lousy gossips. Preparing the house for the solstice party, placing dozens of tiny raspberry candles in every available nook and cranny, I decide that I have to ask. "How well do you know Madelaine, Ruby? Do you even know what kind of a business she has?"

Ruby laughs. "Of course. She calls it 'The Motivated Professional.' She's a dominatrix. I thought we'd talked about that."

Now Ruby and I talk about a lot of things every single day—the house, the kids, our jobs, my dreams, the sun, the moon, the stars—but I think I'd distinctly recall a conversation about a dominatrix. "A Boulder dominatrix? You're kidding. What's the story?"

Ruby puts her arm around me like I'm child. "She's forty-five, Nita, and she was a lawyer for eighteen years. She couldn't stand the crap she had to deal with and having to kiss ass to everyone, so she bailed and started her 'motivational' business. She does it for a living, a very good living from what I hear, but she also does it for fun in her private life. She can get the truth and improved behavior out of men way better than I can as a therapist. We joke about doing tag-team therapy—I could wear them out talking, then she could take them in the back room and whip it out of them. She doesn't tell a lot of people about her business, obviously, even though it's legal. And you know the guys adore her."

Did I dream this to know it, or did I already know it

somehow and put it into my dream? I tell Ruby about my sushi-with-Tanner dream and she only shrugs and laughs and offers me one of her infernal quotes —"You know what Nabokov said, Nita? 'Reality' is the only word that should always appear in quotes."

A nap before the solstice party, that's what I need. And I decide that if I have to hang out naked at the mall in my dreams instead of at the ocean, I might as well lucid-dream a couple of friends in there with me.

I hold hands with Annie Braverman and Nobeko Graham and we stroll in through the east entrance this time, past the security guard who doesn't even blink at our bare skin, and on into the main atrium which is filled with bright purple hummingbirds flying upside down above the Santa Claus booth. They don't belong here at this time of year—they know this and they smile—they belong way across the Gulf of Mexico.

Annie has her VISA card imprinted on her bare ass, the better to finish her holiday shopping, and Nobeko carries a small leather pouch of coins tied around her tiny bare waist. All three of us wear red patent high heels, as though we are expecting to be invited to tango with Al Pacino at any moment.

My body is now covered in piercings, an entire universe of stars, the Milky Way glittering from my eyebrows down to my toes, and I am the most beautiful thing in the mall. Men stop and make offers to buy me, but I refuse. The manager at Trice Jewelers comes out and asks if he can hire me for the holidays to sit in his display window in the middle of all the diamond rings, but I refuse that too. "I am now a stellar cartographer," I explain, "not some astronomical bimbo for sale."

Annie pulls me away and whispers, "There is a secret passageway over by the McDonald's that takes you down by the Mermaid Cave and through the water system and up into any fountain you care to rise into."

We grab a handful of french fries for energy and sneak down through the trapdoor behind the freezer in McDonald's kitchen. A security guard is chasing behind me, shouting "Rhythm! Rhythm!" as though it were my name, and I stop and turn and shout back at him "Blues! Blues! There are starving children in this world! Make all these people stop shopping!" He freezes in his tracks, and we dive down into the water system and begin to swim.

Red high heels act like flippers if you swim fast enough. I am strong and powerful and in control. I could swim laps in this mall a thousand times and still run a marathon. I could save my mother if I saw her drowning in the waves right in front of me. I could catch tuna and eels for the sushi bar with my bare hands and carry them in my teeth. But Annie makes us follow her and rise up into the main fountain, the one in the center of the mall that people like to throw coins into.

There are a thousand men surrounding the fountain where we float and bounce on top of the jets like tiny plastic ping pong balls. A thousand men! I check, but I don't see Madelaine around anywhere. All of the men are wearing button-down dress shirts and ties but are naked from the waist down, and their cocks are erect and at attention. The lead man has a telescope and he is examining my galaxy of piercings.

"Galileo!" someone cries out, and I think it might be my voice. "I am found!" The men applaud politely and all begin to stroke themselves and sing "Amazing Grace," so Annie and Nobeko and I match them, lying back on the upper level of the fountain, posed with our legs spread, heels propped on the outer wall, looking rather like a set of prone Rockettes. We start coming in perfect order—Annie *one*, Nobeko *two*, me *three: one, two, three; one, two, three; one, two, three*, until the men say "Amen," and begin to ask us to dance.

"I was doing the tango in this dream, Ruby, honest, and I could dance. I could swim too, and I wasn't scared. I feel fresh and new, almost like I've bathed in the fountain of youth. What do you think it all means?"

"Ha," snorts Ruby. "I've never understood why people think we need a fountain of youth—it seems to me what we need in this country is a fountain of smart. What does it mean?—it means you slept through my food preparation, Nita." Ruby smiles as she helps me place the gold snowflakes through the tiny holes in my ears. "But it also means that you are dreaming with enthusiasm again, and I believe that when you can do that, you are ready."

Ready for the walk to the park, perhaps. I wear a gold shirt and black slacks. Ruby wears a long red skirt and a soft white sweater. She holds my hand like I am a child; I have always liked this about her.

The park is festooned with red ribbons and crepe paper and balloons tied to trees; a big bonfire burns off to the left of the stage; Leftover Salmon is on stage and starting to play "Ask the Fish." Annie and Sam are here and I check—Annie says she's barely started her shopping and, no, she always pays cash, not VISA.

I dance. I dance with Ruby and with Annie and with Sam, together and separately. I dance with Madelaine and her men. I dance with the kids. I dance as though Nureyev himself were waiting for me on the sidelines and I am just warming up. I dance down the sidewalks on the way back home, and I have no idea where all the childlike energy is coming from.

In the house we light the Yule log and all of the candles. After we finish eating, Ruby passes out the bells. We tell stories, ringing the bells in between each person's tale to honor their spirit; we salute the cycles of nature; we turn and ring the bells in unison while facing North, East, South, and West. Ruby has enough rituals for a lifetime, and I adore every one of them.

After the kids have crashed, each person, from the oldest to the youngest, speaks his or her vision for the coming year. Ruby's vision is one of peace. Madelaine says, "I envision good behavior for all of us." Sam's vision is for time to write and a book contract for him, along with increased love for Annie. My vision, I say, is only of water. Annie says that she wants to go to Rome. Tanner hopes for more and longer dark nights, snuggling up on Madelaine's lap as he says this, and her other lover Tim agrees, and Madelaine pets them both.

Ruby brings out her crystal flute and begins to play as people drift off to the bedrooms to greet the dawn in their own private ways. Ruby and I have the middle bedroom, and we lie very still as voyeurs in our own house. We can hear Annie and Sam passionately fucking on one side of us, and Madelaine and her boys on the other side—Madelaine is making noises like a very happy woman.

Ruby ties my hands together with her red scarf and begins to count my piercings. "Tomorrow, Nita," she whispers, "we start your birthday breakfast with my first present. Madelaine will pierce you any place you like. . .

yes. . .even your tongue." I kiss Ruby deeply, my tongue filling her mouth, knowing that she knows I probably won't take her up on this, but loving her for offering. "Then, we book that next race in Santa Cruz, and I'll be there every step of the way." Her mouth begins the journey down Cassini's Division to the dark spaces in between, her fingers digging in and exploring, thumb in my cunt and index finger in my ass, rocking me, tongue traveling across the ridges of the tiny gold studs in my cunt lips, swirling, driving, sucking, and as the dawn begins to break, she finds the true route home by the light of my North Star.

It Had To Be You

*T*here is a girl in San Francisco who decided to become mute. *My name is bluenote*, she writes, passing her notepad to the tall, bearded man, *and I can not speak but I can play the saxophone, write poetry with my toes and fuck eighty-one different ways.*

"Well, those are good things," the man replies with a French accent, sitting down on the turquoise blanket next to this lovely, black-haired girl. He eyes the balloons soaring overhead, the crowd of people around the bandstand across the park, the yellow legal pad the girl had been passionately writing on for a half hour while he watched. He tries to look at anything but the unfolding and folding of her long tanned legs and the constant hiking of her flimsy dress that kept him at a distance until he could reach some state of gentlemanly control within his jeans.

She looks at him questioningly, yet kindly, as though he might be a wounded bird dropped from the sky, looks at him with eyes the color of the Celtic Sea, a piercing blue that moves toward green with the shifting sunlight. She carefully folds and rips off a quarter-page of a legal sheet and writes: *What can you do?*

My name is Fabrice, he writes back, *and I am a professor here at the university. I am thirty-seven and originally from Quebec.*

She laughs, with the bright sound of a sudden breeze twinkling through tiny silver wind chimes, and places her bronze toes in his lap directly on top of his cock. *That's boring,* she writes, *and I can hear perfectly, you may speak. I meant, what can you actually do?*

Fabrice pets her toes and considers his worth. Maybe my work? "I can invent synthetic molecules." My hobbies? "I can windsurf . . . I can build things that last, like furniture." My passions? I must have some . . . hard to remember . . . God I *am* boring. He wraps one hand around her delicate ankles. "Why don't you show me how you write with your toes."

bluenote pulls her gauzy white skirt up her thighs and tucks it in between her legs. Fabrice catches a glimpse of black curly hair and smiles at the purity of the day. Placing the blue Pentel roller-ball pen between her big and second toe, bluenote props the pad on his lap and begins to write in long sloping curves:

> *I am going mad from roses*
> *softly falling into darkness*
> *stripped of love*
> *drifting*
> *down*
> *to*
> *the*
> *ground*

"Why?" Fabrice asks, wrapping his hand in her long black hair and pulling her over to sit in his lap like a child. "Why are you stripped of love? How are you able to laugh and play the saxophone and not speak?" He can feel the undertow beginning, the tug that starts at the edge of a man's heart when he finds a girl in need of his strength, the tug that turns into a series of waves like the rise of oncoming orgasm, and then eventually, willing or not, evolves into a tidal force that can take a man right down to places he'd rather not go.

bluenote curls up in his arms as though she belongs there and considers which story to tell this new man. Usually she waits until after she has fucked them at least five different ways before she gets anywhere near the truth. *I went crazy,* she rarely says, *after my lover Sam left me three years ago. I went crazy,* she doesn't say, *because he left me for something evil that I did and I could not get him back. I am still crazy,* she does not add, *because Sam still lives above me in North Beach and I am unable to move, not to mention speak, and if I lie very still in my bed at night I can sometimes hear him with his new girlfriend from Colorado who is bright and happy and has children and seems normal. I can hear them loving each other and fucking each other and laughing and dancing and moving through life like real people, and I am only not crazy,* she should add but won't, *when I play sad, soulful songs on my saxophone every night just before dawn and I know he can hear me even when he's not there, although he mostly ignores me and only nods to me in passing and doesn't even know that I can't speak.*

bluenote looks up at Fabrice and shrugs, never answering out loud, instead running her tongue lightly across his lower lip, often a better answer than anything words have to offer. Language, it has been said, was given us to camouflage our truths.

"I can do one more thing I forgot to mention, sweetheart," Fabrice whispers through her kiss. "I can make a woman come in five minutes with only my mouth, no hands."

Show me, she writes slowly down his neck with her

tongue, and she tosses her long pristine skirt over his head like a blanket. Fabrice lowers hungry lips and tongue down between her legs to black curls and it all begins.

Back in her apartment, bluenote begins to strip for him—*this is one of the eighty-one ways, use only your eyes and watch me to begin*—she writes, using the big computer monitor close to the headboard before she stands up and slips one thin arm from the white dress. Fabrice sits on the bed and tries to focus, but he is quite distracted by the room that he finds himself in—it isn't the blue netting on the ceiling, resembling a tourist restaurant on the Wharf, that gets to him. It isn't all the fish tanks, or the big rattan basket filled with pieces of cut rope and a book on Japanese rope bondage, it isn't even the one wall covered with little white slips of paper from what looks like a lifetime's worth of fortune cookies—it's the other wall, the one covered with snakes.

Don't worry about the snakes, she had written with a laugh when he first entered the room and stopped cold. *They just watch.*

There are some images that a man will never forget. Fabrice watches bluenote put on the music, a slow Leonard Cohen song about dancing until the end of love. He watches her begin to dance, watches the big orange, black and white snakes displayed like artwork in shaky-looking cages on the wall behind her, and he desperately tries to recall the name and color of every poisonous snake he's ever heard of, all while smiling at the lovely girl who is offering herself to him.

Images at dusk: sunlight fading, shades of gray, shadows on the wall, candles lit, the thin undulating body of the girl as she drops her dress on the floor near the window, this gift of a girl with the long black hair that flows over her small breasts, this girl who is left standing in only a white lace camisole and white lace-up sandals. She moves toward him, offering her body for inspection, bending backward in front of him and parting her pussy lips to show him her softness; she holds her small brown nipples out for him, pinching them, watching him react.

Come, strip for me, she motions to Fabrice as the song changes, pulling him to his feet and unbuttoning his shirt. He tries to move like she does. As he removes his shirt and she circles around him, the world ceases to exist outside the room. She moves her lips in tune with the song with no words to be heard—"I remember when I moved in you and the holy dove she was moving too and every breath that I drew was hallelujah . . ." Even with her sandals on, she barely comes up to his chin; he thinks perhaps he could lift her up and carry her away and keep her in a cage of his own, and no one would ever know.

She unbuttons the fly on his jeans and runs her fingers down inside, tangling through his thick pubic hair and bringing his cock out for her inspection. She smiles. *I forgot to tell you this,* he thinks to himself, *this is something I can do. I can offer you what women say is a very long cock, long and curved, not terribly thick, but a cock that reaches every place that needs to be reached.*

bluenote pauses and motions toward the wall—*it's like a snake.*

A baby snake, maybe, he thinks, suddenly insecure given the other images in the room. He turns away from the snake wall to focus on his next move.

He lowers his jeans, removes every stitch of clothing, and stands naked in front of her, trying to hold on to her arms and keep her close to him, but she keeps slithering away, dancing, running her hands through her hair and down her body, dipping her fingers into her pussy and licking them clean. She moves like a belly-dancer except she has no real hips to speak of, nothing much to hold onto as she twirls around him, until she lands at his feet. Looking up at him with those eyes, she begins to climb up his body, wrapping around his legs, kissing and licking her way up and around, from his cock to his ass and back again.

bluenote picks up a long piece of rope from the basket, stands close to Fabrice, and begins to wrap it around her leg, then around his leg, weaving them together. "You're tying us together," he murmurs brightly, standing very still and watching the artwork of the rope running around his balls, between his legs, straight across her pussy, and then back down her leg. bluenote nods and stands up, wrapping her arms around his chest like a child standing on top of her father's shoes ready to be walked up the stairs. She lifts her free leg up and over his cock until it's positioned between her legs. Her wetness flows over him and he understands that she wants him to enter her and continue dancing with her this way, his cock deep inside her, deep, deeper, driving her up to his lips every time they move. Moving together in exact rhythm, leaning, turning, spinning, pausing, thrusting; the night begins to last forever.

There are some things that happen in a moment that take a lifetime to explain. Exhausted, spent, lying head to toe on the bed, untied but still entangled, bluenote stretches to get a piece of paper from the nightstand and writes—*I hope you don't mind, but I always sleep with Flow, my favorite snake. He protects me.* Fabrice says nothing, finds no words to protest, and then somehow it seems a reasonable thing to do: to fall asleep with the legs of a beautiful young girl you just met in the park wrapped around you and a snake you'd rather not meet wrapped around her.

At precisely 4:30 a.m. bluenote wakes Fabrice up and asks him to leave. She picks a fortune from the wall as he leaves and gives it to him with a kiss. He pauses to read it in his car: "You can kiss and fix whatever's wrong but no one stays kissed for very long."

bluenote watches from her bay window as Fabrice drives away in his little black Fiat. Playing "Body and Soul" on her saxophone at dawn, she sees her neighbor Sam across the street, strapping his duffel bag on the back of his motorcycle. It's hard to tell what Sam is up to by looking at him—he's the kind of guy who wears the same black leather jacket and packs the same bag whether he is going to Colorado or Japan. But even though she has not spoken to Sam for almost three years, bluenote knows exactly where he is going and for how long. Sam Davidoff: ex-lover, upstairs neighbor, tall, dark-haired, bespectacled, smart, worldly journalist; Sam Davidoff, cruel, cold, distant, gone; Sam Davidoff: the point of every obsessive note she has ever played, the man who was meant to be hers.

It's not really stalking because he loved me. Besides, I don't do anything bad, not anymore. bluenote reaches into Flow's cage to retrieve a key, the copy of the key to Sam's apartment that she has had ever since the breakup, the key Sam has no idea she still has since she has become invisible to him. She takes out the key, wraps Flow around her neck, picks up a piece of cord from the basket and adds it to her snake-necklace. *He's just forgotten he loved me. There have been a hundred men since Sam, but I can't remember any of their faces, though I certainly can remember the snake and the tongue of the man from last night. It's not stalking, because I love Sam and I would never hurt him. He was going to marry me once.* She goes outside and up the back stairs and lets herself into his apartment quietly.

Rituals and patterns create clarity. There are self-made rules and bluenote follows them. First, she checks Sam's calendar to see what's coming up, then she reads all of his downloaded email to find out how his life is going. *I would never actually hack his password and log onto his account, that would be a bad thing. I only did a bad thing once, when I gave his cat away. But I was so angry back then. And I did find him a good home.* She reads the latest installments of both his novel and his play, resisting the urge to edit. Standing up, she strips off her dress, drops it onto his bed, goes to his closet and chooses one of his big white button-down shirts to wear. Leaving the shirt open, she sits on his bed and ties her ankles together and then ties the rope to his bedpost. Flow wraps around her leg, and then she lies back across his big brass bed and begins to remember and dream.

bluenote strokes her legs, letting Flow wrap around and around her and tries to relive her last real night with Sam, tries to create in her dreams how it could have been.

If I dream it just right it will be different. "I understand why you had an abortion while I was gone," he would whisper kindly to me, "and I understand that you got sterilized while you were at it, because you thought I truly didn't want kids like you don't." He would stroke my shoulders, my face, my tears, he would tell me he loved me anyway. "I understand," he would continue, "that you weren't really being sneaky, that you didn't contact me in Japan because you were upset and scared and thought I might be proud of you even though you know that we agreed you weren't to do anything drastic in your life ever again without discussing it with me," and he would cover my body with his bulk and hold me down on the bed the way I needed him to, and he would tell me over and over again, "It's OK, I love you, Kendall my sweet bluenote, it's OK, it's just an unexpected twist of fate and we can handle it. I love you". . and he would crawl right up into my body and fuck me hard into the bed and all the words would have meaning and I would never again in my life have anyone or anything else inside of me except for Sam.

bluenote begins to come, shivering and shaking and crying on top of the bed with the force of memory and possibilities, but she is sad, as always, to open her eyes and find that it is still only she and Flow keeping Sam's bed warm.

Rituals and patterns create clarity. After she comes, bluenote hangs Sam's slightly wrinkled shirt back up, gets dressed, eats a bite of food from his refrigerator, brushes her teeth with his toothbrush and proceeds to scrub his bathroom for him—a small act of contrition. She leaves his apartment and locks the door, tucking the fortune she has brought for him under his doormat—*you will attend a royal banquet and remember what you already knew.* She whispers the only word that still sounds right in her throat— "Sam"—and goes back downstairs.

"You should have a party, Sam," his lover, Annie Braverman, says when visiting him in June. "You're always happy when I have them in Boulder. At least let's have a dinner party—you're a great cook. We could fit six people here—and let's invite that sad-looking girl that lives downstairs, the one you used to go out with, so maybe she'll stop staring at me out her window like I'm poison. She must have a boyfriend to bring."

Sam and Annie are wrapped together in his deep old-fashioned bathtub, soaking beneath the bath oils and bubbles that Annie never travels without. Sam is holding her leg up in the air and slowly shaving it for her, one of the ways she's convinced him to not be such a guy and just shower all the time.

He looks at her hard when she suggests the party. Annie has begun to fill up every available empty space in his life—his bathtub, his apartment, his writing, his heart. Somehow she makes him do things he hadn't even thought of doing. Already, thanks to her suggestion to do something about the problems in the world, he's "adopted" three poor kids in Appalachia through some children's group and keeps their pictures on his fridge. She's made him try snowboarding, she's made him learn tantric sex, she's made him laugh more than he'd ever laughed before—even as a kid—and she's managed to make him recognize the word "dream" again, a word he likes to edit out of every story that comes across his desk.

How to tell her? "The girl downstairs is named Kendall, and I haven't spoken to her in several years. I'm surprised she hasn't moved away. All I remember about her is that she was a good writer, mostly poetry, and that she worked at home and was starting to do some kind of research on the Web for a living. She used to have a snake in her apartment, and she used to take care of my cat Maxie for me before he ran away." What else to share? "I hardly see her because of the separate entrances in the building. She was a little upset when we broke up, a long time ago. Let's not include her for dinner. I've seen her with a lot of different men over time, and I'm sure she's happy. But she was always a little crazy around the edges."

"Aren't we all, Sam," Annie offers, rising from the bubbles and floating up to stretch out and press her bare body on top of his in the water and kiss him softly. "Aren't we all." She turns over, lies with her back to his chest and begins to kiss him with a reverse kiss—a kiss she hasn't mentioned she learned at a party once where almost everything was better than sex, a kiss that is as simple as turning your head and kissing sort of backwards in a way that makes the person you're kissing look and feel entirely different than the basic eye-to-eye kiss, a kiss that starts on the lips and travels to the tongue and then back to concentrate on the sucking of the bottom lip, sucking until the victim is moaning with pleasure. Annie moves down through the water to his chin, to his neck, to his nipples, and she stays there for a very long time, moving from one of his nipples to another and sucking and biting until his nipples are bright red and standing at an attention that could rival his cock.

Sam closes his eyes, moans, and runs his hands up through her long, tangled, wet hair. "Annie, Annie. Do you know, I'll do anything for you . . . "

Annie smiles and lies on top of him again, with her back to his chest and begins to slide his hard cock inside of her, wrapping her strong legs down and underneath him, sliding slowly up and down against his body, fucking him in exquisite slow motion, breaking from another reverse kiss to whisper, "Then a dinner party it is. It will be good for you, darlin'—and besides, I like girls who like snakes."

bluenote and Fabrice arrive for dinner promptly at seven on Saturday night, joining Annie, Sam, and two of Sam's favorite editors, Howard and Hannah. Several bottles of wine are offered up by Howard and Hannah. bluenote brings tea, and oranges, and says that they came all the way from China.

bluenote wears a long red sleeveless dress with big pockets and carries a half-sized legal pad and pen in one pocket. When Annie asks her what kind of work she does, she writes, *I research words on the Net—lyrics, poetry, fortune cookies.*

"Fortune cookies?"

Yes, specialty fortune cookies. I help write them too, but all sayings have to be cleared for copyright. GenX Cookies, Atheist Cookies, Random Song Cookies, X-Rated Cookies, of course, Over-the-Hill Cookies, Chicken Soup Cookies, and more.

Annie laughs as she reads bluenote's words and asks about her favorite fortunes, but she notices that Sam is watching and listening from the kitchen while chatting off and on with Howard, who is helping him cook. Sam has been almost completely silent since the girl arrived and Fabrice explained to everyone that she could hear but not speak. As they begin to serve the cous cous, Sam is beginning to remember three things he had forgotten he knew about bluenote: that up close she is strikingly beautiful in a sensitive, fragile-waif kind of way; that she has eyes a man can get lost in; and that everything she says must be examined for shades of the truth.

At dinner, Fabrice talks about his new after-hours work project—researching speech patterns and communication. "bluenote is psychologically mute, a condition more common than I had realized before meeting her this spring," he explains. "I figure if my lab can make synthetic molecules that profit rich drug companies, I can surely use the same research skills to help one woman regain her speech."

bluenote laughs and shrugs and rolls her eyes, as though to excuse Fabrice's devotion. She writes a note for him to read to everyone at the table. *I don't need to speak. Everyday language is highly overrated. I can do more interesting things than speak—I can play the saxophone, write poetry with my toes and fuck eighty-one different ways.*

"Eighty-one?" says Annie, barely missing a beat. "Wow, that's great. I only know maybe sixty-two, and I've studied the *Kama Sutra* forever. We need to compare notes."

"The number eighty-one," Fabrice explains as though this is important, "is one of those 'magic multiples' of nine—products, sum of the digits, the works. bluenote loves ritual and precision."

"Not to mention," says Hannah, "that 81 is a number that can be turned top to bottom and still maintain its identity."

Everyone laughs away the awkward moment, but Sam stares hard at bluenote, trying to determine how much of this is an act for him and how much might be true, a position he remembers finding himself in way more than once many years ago. "Kendall," he says, a bit sharply, speaking to her directly for the first time since saying hello at his front door, "maybe after dinner you can entertain us with these things."

bluenote stands up and clears her plate, making herself right at home in Sam's apartment, almost as though she lived there. She comes back to him, leans over his shoulder, and writes—*entertain you with the eighty-one ways?*

"No. The music, the fortunes, the poetry, the toes—all the remarkable things you can do."

When she presses into his shoulder, her intense scent is immediately familiar to Sam—she has always worn men's colognes, Old English or Brut, which smell entirely different on a woman—and he slips away to pour more wine rather than recall anything else.

I'd be glad to provide any of my talents for tonight's entertainment . . . but I'm being so rude, bluenote writes, turning toward Annie and the others. *Tell me, what can* **you** *do?*

Everyone has something to offer. Howard begins. "I can speak some Japanese. I can tango. I won a yo-yo championship in college and can still 'walk the dog,' do 'around the world,' you name it. But, Hannah . . . Hannah can sing like an angel."

Hannah smiles genuinely, but with a certain distance. "I'm still in process about my singing. Something I *can* do is act like the Red Queen and imagine six impossible things before breakfast every day."

"Impossible things, yes. A good plan," agrees Fabrice, with his arm around bluenote. "Personally, I can tell you exactly how many steps it takes to cross the Golden Gate Bridge. bluenote makes me walk across it with her all the time. I lived here for ten years and never once set foot on the bridge 'til I met her. I have to say, she's made me much less boring than I was when we first met."

Even Sam laughs at that.

Your turn, Annie, bluenote writes.

"Well, let's see. I can stand on my head for an hour."

So can I, bluenote writes quickly in response, turning to face Annie and looking at her expectantly, pen poised to respond.

"I can beat Sam at chess."

So can I.

"I can talk with my cats.

I can talk to my snakes, we speak the same language. What else?

Annie laughs and considers. "Well, I can dance with my cat, Zenrose. Sometimes she even leads."

bluenote smiles smugly. *I can dance with snakes. Want to try it?*

When Annie agrees to go downstairs to see bluenote's snakes, everyone else accompanies them, albeit with some reluctance. After one peek at the wall of cages, Hannah suggests to Howard that they really should leave because it is so late, and she needs to be fresh for impossibilities the next morning.

Sam stays, entranced by all that he sees. Ropes, the book about bondage, mementos that he recognizes as his, a wall of fortunes on which he reads several of his own statements, including: "Never say you're sorry for things that you can't control," two dozen snakes arranged like art on a museum wall. He walks around the room for a long time and finally sits on the edge of the bed and watches Annie and bluenote together.

"They're not dangerous," Fabrice is assuring Annie. "These are called Louisiana snakes, and they only look like the poisonous Coral snakes." bluenote hands the first snake to Annie, who bravely holds it out in front of her.

"Are you sure?" Annie asks a bit tentatively.

bluenote nods.

"Really?" Annie tries to bring the snake a little closer.

"Of course," Fabrice answers with a laugh. "Believe me, I had the same question when I first came here, but I've learned to trust bluenote completely."

bluenote wraps two of the smaller snakes around each of her bare arms and beckons Annie to do the same. *They're like bracelets*, Annie says to herself, *that's all*, and follows suit, shivering from her bare shoulders in her halter dress down to her now bare feet. Fabrice has lit candles and put on music, some kind of West African high-life music, sophisticated, but still primal, music that makes dancing with snakes by the flickering light in this strange girl's apartment seem like a sane thing to do.

bluenote hikes her long red dress up and ties it at her hip. She dances over to Sam, twirling, arms undulating high above her head, waving her hands around his head, snakes inches from his face, teasing him, rubbing her leg up against his, watching him never flinch. She dances to Fabrice, to Annie, back to Sam, and even Annie has forgotten the snakes on her own arms as she watches the way bluenote can move.

Dance with me, bluenote beckons to Annie and they begin together, arms intertwined, hips rotating, bluenote slinking down to the floor and helping Annie tie her own long black skirt up at her hip also on the way back up, baring one leg. *One more snake,* bluenote motions and finds Flow and lets him wrap himself from Annie's ankle up to her thigh. *Dance for Fabrice,* she instructs, and Annie begins to try to move the way she does, and twirls around Fabrice who stands and takes her hand to guide her.

bluenote wraps snakes on her neck, her legs, her waist and returns to Sam. *Do you remember,* she asks him with her eyes, *you were the man who taught me to feel this way.* He sits very still on the edge of the bed; she moves slowly, pressing in between his legs, stroking his cheek, watching him want to get up and leave, but he appears hypnotized and unable to move. *Do you remember,* she asks him with her body, with her knee pressing firmly up against his crotch, *do you remember how I can make you feel, do you remember the things we tried with the snake, do you remember the things you did to me?* bluenote glances toward Annie dancing at Fabrice's feet with his hand in her hair, and leans into Sam, pressing him back toward the headboard, climbing up over him and straddling him, dancing with her skirt fully lifted, snakes crawling, music pounding, and Sam finally turns his head away to try and clear it, and what he sees looped around her bedpost near the pillow stops him cold.

Sam grabs bluenote by the arm and pushes her off of him and onto the floor. He holds the little green cat collar with the brass bell up in front of her face and doesn't say a word. He drops the collar in her lap and looks around the room one more time; looks in her eyes and sees what he never wanted to know; looks to Annie who has stopped dancing for Fabrice and is watching him closely. He stands up, straightens his clothing, and begins to walk away.

bluenote regains her composure and motions to Fabrice. "Wait," says Fabrice, doing his best to interpret. "Maybe it's time for Sam to tell us what he can do . . ."

Sam pauses and turns, with a look that scares even Annie. "What can I do? I can leave." The door slams behind him.

Twenty-nine million cars go across the Golden Gate Bridge each year and well over a thousand people have jumped off of it to their deaths. On Sunday afternoon, Annie, bluenote, Fabrice and Flow stand on the east-side pedestrian walk looking over the railing. Flow is wrapped safely around bluenote's neck, underneath her jacket.

"I used to come here all the time too, when I lived here a long time ago," Annie says. "It's the most popular public place in the world for suicide. The Eiffel Tower is the second." Annie holds bluenote's hand tightly. "I had considered Paris."

Why? bluenote writes.

"Who knows? It seemed so intensely important at the time. I was miserable. Some man broke my heart. I was obsessed with that loss. I was empty. I couldn't feel anything. Do you know that at least twenty-five people have jumped off this bridge and survived the jump? And that none of them who have been interviewed ever even tried to kill themselves again? Most said they regretted it the second they left the bridge. Things change. Chaos subsides. Time alters our existence—one day out of the blue I learned that there was joy in the world and it was mine for the taking if only I would pay attention and reach for it. I guess it's like the song says, "Once in a while you get shown the light/in the strangest of places if you look at it right."

bluenote smiles a weak smile and writes quickly. *Decisions made too fast seem to be the ones that last. I would come here every day after Sam told me to be quiet, and I would consider how the cold water might feel. I'd wear my long cape and sometimes I'd tie myself to that railing over there, always carrying my camera so people would leave me alone. Then I started bringing Flow. How could I jump without him? How could I jump with him? He saved my life. I just stopped talking instead. It makes the world a softer place. Nobody ever yells at you when you can't speak.*

Fabrice wraps his arms around bluenote and holds her tight and tells her he loves her.

It's been harder to keep up my obsession since I met you, Fabrice. You distract me with your kindness.

"I am focused on you, sweetheart, and you will learn to do the same with me. Even if I have to tie you directly to my heart."

Tuesday morning in the hour before dawn: Annie is asleep, but Sam isn't, awakened, he realizes, by the silence —by the absence of bluenote's saxophone. He hears a scratching at the door. Sam pads quietly through the apartment, opens the door and finds his long-missing cat Maxie there, her green collar intact, the key to his apartment hanging from her collar, a little white fortune attached to the key: *It's never too late for another simple twist of fate.*

Barcelona Girls

They say that lust is a deadly sin, but how could this be so? Lust keeps you alive, starts your day, ends your night, brings you love and keeps your passion bright. Perhaps God could replace the sin of lust with something wiser still—say, overuse of the remote control? Lust creates children, breeds devotion, inspires great music, brings you to your knees, writes lyrical poems of joy and madness and sets your spirit free. Who ever wrote a sonnet about television?

A Visit From the Virtues

"*T*urn off the television, Jack. I need to tell you my dream."

China reaches her pale freckled arm across the bed playfully toward Jack, swipes the remote and flicks the TV off. Each morning since they've arrived on their vacation at Club Med near Barcelona, Jack has picked up the odd new habit of rising early, too early for China, running on the beach, disappearing for hours, then returning to flip

131

on the tube and awaken her with the less than romantic sounds of nattering daytime television.

"I'm all sweaty, China. I need to shower . . . you know I'm just running to fend off the gluttony and sloth of hanging around here for two weeks, " he tells her, not for the first time. She suspects that he's actually avoiding all sort of things, including her. "I know it's a lucky assignment," Jack continues, "to be here on a free vacation in return for my photography, but still. This place is deadly for me."

"Jack," she whispers, throwing the covers off their king-sized canopy bed, "pay attention."

China's long, wavy, pale red hair hangs loose over her small breasts, her hair still tangled from tossing and turning all night, her eyes still hazy from dreaming. "There's no such thing as greed or gluttony when it comes to sex, Jack, you taught me that. I love you so much," she whispers. She can only vaguely remember how shy she used to be about her body when she first met Jack, even wearing long flannel shirts to bed with him on occasion. She climbs up on top of him, takes the ponytail band out of his long hair, pulls off his shorts, straddles him and begins to gently pet his soft cock. "Do you know that every night in my sleep I dream you perfectly into being?"

Jack groans as she moves on top of him, kissing his lips, his neck, his ears. *She's so beautiful and trusting. I could never tell her what's going on . . . never follow through on my instructions from that woman—my . . . Mistress. Madelaine. Darkstar. Whoever she thinks she is. I'll never tell China why we're really here . . . never do anything else that might betray her faith.* "OK, tell me your dream, China. I'm all yours."

China smiles and runs her hands down his body. "Well, we were in a castle, like that one we saw yesterday outside of Figueras, and there was a stone floor and we were sleeping on it for some reason. I think it was some kind of dungeon. I heard other voices in the room, but I couldn't see anyone, and I didn't care because I woke up wanting you . . . like this." She slides down between his legs and gently kisses the tip of his cock.

"My hands ran down over your shoulders and your arms, over your hips, caressing your legs and your belly, making your body turn toward me in half-sleep. My lips followed my hands, gently kissing every inch of you awake . . . like this."

A very long pause with no words. Then —"I wanted to spend hours that way—tasting you, kissing you, devouring you, drawing strength from you, teasing you and loving you. I was sure you were awake, but you kept your eyes closed and let me take care of you."

Jack closes his eyes and gives in to her voice, her touch, forgetting everything else.

"It felt like the whole world was watching and the voices in the distance were getting louder, but I still didn't care. Your cock started to harden under my lips . . . like this . . I climbed between your legs, spreading them gently with my hands, and I heard you moan with pleasure."

Jack moans, on cue.

"My mouth worked its way down over your balls, softly licking back and forth from your ass up to your cock, taking your growing cock in my mouth, then letting it go, caressing your balls with my tongue and my mouth, holding your legs wide with my hands and stroking your thighs. My tongue found your asshole, and entered it gently, licking and probing . . . like this."

Jack spreads a little wider.

"Then I heard another woman speak! She said, quite loudly, 'YOU HAVE TO SHARE HIM WITH US.'"

Jack opens his eyes quickly and looks around, jerked out of his sensual reverie by the implication and a bit of nervousness.

"So I looked up in my dream and there were seven women circled around us on the stone floor. 'No,' I said, 'he's mine,' and they all just smiled at me like they knew everything there was to know. They each had a flashing bright sign above their heads, the words sort of floating and flashing their names, kind of like a shiny halo name tag. 'FAITH,' it said above the girl who was talking to me, and she looked a bit like Donna Reed, wearing pearls and everything, except she was stark naked like they all were. She held hands with a girl with long blonde hair and very big breasts whose sign said "JUSTICE . . FOR ALL."

Hope Takes a Turn

"I ignored them, hoping they would go away," China whispers. "I straddled your leg . . . like this . . . and wrapped myself around you . . . like this . . . and you could feel the dripping wetness of my pussy pressed against you, rubbing uncontrollably against your leg as my tongue left your asshole—replaced by my finger—and trailed back up toward your stiff cock . . . like this . . . my mouth could resist no longer and I took your hard cock within my lips, just the head at first, running my tongue around the rim, sucking and licking and tasting you . . . like this." China is mumbling now. "I took your cock in slowly, inch by inch, until all of it was deep in my throat. I held it there for a minute and then started to slowly work my way up and down, in and out, never letting go completely, pushing my finger into your ass in rhythm with my mouth, feeling your body give into me all the way . . . "

The storytelling stops for a while, and Jack debates whether to flip over and fuck China the way she likes, or to leave her in control. She slides his cock out of her mouth before he can decide.

"Your hands were in my hair, Jack . . . like this . . . and there were still no words spoken between us. There was nothing but your cock and my mouth, my own wetness dripping down your leg as my excitement peaked . . . like this . . . and then the girl named Hope tapped me on the shoulder and said, 'MY TURN.'"

Jack laughs and wonders if perhaps he's the one dreaming.

"Suddenly it seemed the charitable thing to do, to share you. You didn't seem to mind. I moved over and offered Hope your other leg to straddle and let her start sucking your cock. You were paying very close attention then. We began to lick your cock up and down in rhythm like two little girls sharing our special ice cream cone, and then another girl tapped me on the other shoulder and asked to cut in. 'Please do,' I said, and I backed off to watch. 'SLOWLY, SLOWLY,' the girl named Temperance said, and the other girls circled closer around you until they could all touch you and kiss you and lick you."

Jack's eyes are open, but China's are closed as she alternates between speaking and attending to his cock.

"As you got close to coming, you stopped them all and you said, 'Let China fuck me now.' They lifted me up, wordlessly, spreading my legs wide, holding my hips, sliding my wet pussy onto the tip of your cock . . . like this. 'Fuck me, China,' you said, and, 'FUCK HIM GIRL,' they said, and I lost control, sliding my pussy down completely, taking your cock deep inside me, feeling your hands on my hips and my waist and their hands all over me, lifting me back up and then down hard on your cock again, both of us feeling the orgasm near . . . "

"Like this, baby, like this," Jack says, lifting her up and down as she whispers the words.

"Yes, yes . . . your cock exploded inside of me, and all

the girls sighed, and we rocked back and forth together, my body pressed on top of yours, lying together in the morning sun as though we were one, not nine . . . "

"Like this, baby, like this," Jack repeats, and they come together in the morning sun that streams through the window, Jack kissing her long and softly, silencing the words, until he thinks she's almost asleep.

She stirs in his arms. "But there's a little more, Jack—the girls politely turned their neon lights off and faded back into the stone walls. I realized that I liked sharing you and hoped they would return."

Jack whispers bravely, "Well, if you liked that dream, China, you might like the . . . uh . . . 'cocktail party' we're invited to Friday night at Madelaine's, the woman I'm photographing for. She said it will be all women—except for me. And she wants to meet you. You've seemed a little sad lately—maybe this will cheer you up. Or . . . maybe not."

"That's funny, Jack. That's sort of what the girl named Prudence warned me of in my dream. Just before she turned out her light, she whispered, "Be careful—sadness used to be the eighth deadly sin, you know. Beware of bare women gifting Jack.""

Darkstar, Rising

The next morning, the woman named Madelaine sits on the beach, writing and waiting for Jack, while two men attend to her. She is tall, with short cropped black hair, laughing eyes and large tanned bare breasts. Dressed only in a black bikini bottom, she exudes confidence from every pore. Fortyish, she is not exactly pretty, but striking in a smart and powerful way, a woman that inspires curiosity at first sight. The younger man, Tanner, sits at her feet and polishes her toenails. The older man, Jerry, sits on her far side and simply holds her drink.

"What will you call your book, Mistress?" Tanner asks between strokes of the brush.

She laughs, a throaty, knowing laugh. "It's just my private journal, you know that, my sweet slave. But if I published it, I could change all the names to protect the less than innocent and call it, 'Chicken Soup for the Kinky Soul.' True stories of inspiration for my fellow deviants."

As she considers what she will do with Jack today when he finally arrives, she flips through the pages of her journal and reads to herself:

A man has to sign a detailed contract before I will touch him. I'm a lawyer by training, a dominatrix by passion and lust. But pick a title— Dominatrix, Domina, Domme, Mistress, Goddess—all of them beat the hell out of "attorney-at-law." Most men I am close to just call me Darkstar. My business card is serious though. It reads: Madelaine Penafiel, President, The Motivated Professional. I *am* serious. I don't just fulfill men's fantasies of being overpowered and brought to their knees — I can actually make a man a better person. Sort of like the Promise Keepers, only with a whip.

My newest client, Jack Iverson, passed the initial interview back in Colorado four months ago and had the privilege of signing a contract with me. "Jack," I asked him as he knelt in the center of his studio in our first session, fully dressed, hands clasped behind his waist, "did you read all of the fine print?"

"Of course, Ma'am."

Nobody calls me ma'am, that makes me sound too much like somebody's mother—although it is true that domming men is a mix of playing kinky bitch and mothering them.

"No, dear. You will call me Mistress Dark," I told him.

I circled him, the four-inch heels on my silver thigh-high boots clicking on his tile floor. Those boots hurt like hell. But they're about the only way in which I condescend to fulfill the expected image during a session. Men love the boots, adore them, worship them. They take them off for me, they put them on me, they polish them, they massage my feet, lick my toes, bathe my feet with their tongues—all while anticipating the sight of me back in the boots and standing over them, my spikes threatening everything they've got.

In our first session, I ran my riding crop lightly across Jack's back, over his cheek and beard, down his chest. I knew from the look on his face that he had never read the contract. He was clearly the kind of guy who always thinks he's getting away with something. "I'm the one really in control," is what I read in his eyes. His studio told me everything else I needed to know about him: Lots of expensive photo equipment, a few good framed shots, canvasses covered with cobwebs, books, magazines, Nintendo—lots of trivial distractions available in every direction—a man with permanent potential, but no discipline.

"If you read the contract, slave, what is your safeword to be?"

"Safeword?"

I had him read me the entire contract out loud from start to finish. When he got to the clause,

"Your safeword will be 'China,' like the country," he paused for only a second. "A safeword means 'STOP,'" the contract explained. "It doesn't mean 'no,' or 'I don't like that,' it means 'stop everything immediately,' with no explanations necessary. It's the single tiny piece of control you have over this arrangement."

After we finished with the contract, I had him strip down and stand before me for examination. "Mistress Dark, do I please you?" he asked in an uncharacteristically shy voice.

I love men's bodies. Hell, I love men, which is certainly not true for everyone who does what I do. I spent years searching for my true sexuality, only to discover that I am simply an oversexed bisexual pervert who needs to control men. This is fortunate, since men will pay anything for what I can do to them.

Don Juan Learns a Lesson

"Your body does please me, slave," I told Jack as I circled him, tapping, touching, pinching, prodding—I was particularly pleased by his muscled thighs and the thick, hard cock that was begging for my touch.

I slid on my latex gloves, and he looked like he might come just at the sight of my hands. I made him suck my fingers slowly, one by one, and watched as he began to go under, began to head toward the place that's called "sub-space," a hypnotic state of mind where pleasure and pain intermix and one often becomes the other. The avoidance of pain and the seeking of pleasure cause most of the personal problems in the world, and I know how to alter someone's reality. It's a powerful position for me to be in, and I treat it with respect. I sure would like to get hold of someone like, say, Bill Clinton, though, and teach him how to behave in ten easy lessons. If there is ever an obvious candidate for a dominatrix, it's an oversexed, smart, talented man who's out of control in his daily life.

Like Jack. My scene with him started out as a favor to a friend. I was visiting Annie Braverman at her Halloween party in Boulder when we saw this cute long-haired guy dressed as Don Juan hitting on every woman in sight. "Now that," she said, "is a man in need of better behavior. I adore his girlfriend China and think he needs to shape up fast." The negotiations between Annie and me were quick—a dare, a tease: I'd take Jack on, and she'd pay for his sessions, but only if I proved that I can truly improve a man's behavior in quantifiable ways. I think perhaps she doubted me.

I have Jack keep a ledger of his assignments, the improvements I tell him to work on week by week. Pretend you're like Ben Franklin, I tell him, who used to work exclusively on one virtue a week, making little x marks every time he "sinned." Jack doesn't need to know about the dare; he only knows about our direct trade: my kink for his photography services. He gets to be turned on and improve his life; I get good pictures, payment from Annie, and further confirmation of my own sexual prowess—it's a win/win kink situation. Anyone who thinks this kind of sex work is evil should seriously reconsider—the most important "sin" I observe every day is the failure to imagine and live out your very own life as it was meant to be.

When Jack finished sucking my last finger in that first session, I had him stand at attention with his legs spread apart, tied his hands behind his back with a long rope and pulled up a high stool in front of him. I lifted my short silver skirt and let him watch me finger my own full black bush while I talked to him about what I expected. He couldn't take his eyes off my fingers. I'm forty-six years old and men of all ages worship my cunt—I'd say this beats the hell out of practicing law.

I ran the long rope hanging behind him from his wrists through his spread legs and up to his cock. I took a long time wrapping his cock and balls; he got harder and harder by the minute, as I knew he would, but I told him he could not come yet. Once he was bound to perfection, I had him bend over, smacked his ass with the riding crop until he was moaning, shoved my gloved finger up his ass, and watched him come all over his hardwood floor.

"Next time, you'll be naked and kneeling when I arrive," I told him after he was unbound and laid out on the sofa with a glass of water. "And, sweetheart—clean this place up and make it worthy of me."

It was. He was more than eager on my second visit. I let him kneel between my legs and use only his tongue to make me come over and over again. Technically I don't have sex with my paying men, but we've all heard that oral sex isn't technically sex anyway.

Each session after that grew in intensity and strictness. "Eventually," I would promise him, "if you're good enough, you'll be allowed to visit one of my dungeons." I didn't know if I'd really go that far with him. In fact, I had considered letting him go after a few months to get back to his real life, my point proven, but then I got a good look at the fabled red-headed China, Jack's girlfriend, and all my plans changed.

Six Impossible Things Before Breakfast

Jack arrives at Darkstar's chair on the sand, out of breath from the long run down the beach.

"Kiss my feet," she orders him, dismissing her other two men with a wave of her hand.

Jack obeys, kneeling in the sand and kissing her tanned feet, careful to avoid the fresh nail polish.

"Make me laugh."

This order is always the hardest for Jack to obey, and she always starts off with it—he considers himself a funny guy, but it's next to impossible to make someone laugh on command. Still, he tries. He can't explain the control she has over him, but by now she's so far inside his head that he's lost track of the word 'no.'

"I've been writing some limericks for you, Mistress— here's one:

> There was a great Mistress named Dark
> Whose rules were no walk in the park
>   But if walk said she
>   On a leash I would be
> And for her I would even . . . bark."

Darkstar laughs for only a quick second. "Do it. Bark."

He looks around, sees no one but Tanner and Jerry in the distance, and obeys, as quietly as possible.

She pats his head. "Good boy. You'll do anything for me. Did you tell China yet?"

"Well . . . yes. She'll come on Friday."

"Excellent. Have her wear a white dress."

"Yes, Mistress," Jack answers, considering just how he'll handle the introduction — "China, this is my secret dominatrix, Madelaine Penafiel, the only other woman in the world who thinks I might actually be an artist, particularly when she has me tied up and begging," probably wouldn't go over too well.

"But . . . I can't serve you while she's there, Mistress."

Darkstar pulls Jack closer to her, his head on her lap. "I know you remember, dear, that *can't* is a word we reserve for the physically impossible—like you can't swim across this sea to Rome before dinner time tonight. But, don't worry, you won't serve me directly. Perhaps you'll serve China instead."

He tries to imagine this, but can only imagine serving China something like breakfast, which reminds him that she's patiently waiting for him back at their room, hopefully after a night with no further portentous dreams.

"What is China's fantasy, Jack?"

"Fantasy? I don't know—me, I suppose."

Darkstar laughs. "Now, that's funny. You're an attractive man, Jack, but I've never known a woman who didn't have a fantasy way beyond her real-life lover. Pay attention. Find out by tomorrow morning." She holds up one of her large breasts and offers him her nipple. "Make me feel it."

She leans back in the morning sun to watch. Jack places his hands behind his waist as required and begin to suck on her nipple with a practiced mouth while she wraps her fist in his long hair to help guide him. There is so much to sex that has so little to do with actual sex. All of Darkstar's

143

men get off on the small things—the words, the sucking, the touching, the obedience. And like all of them, if she tells Jack to stay there and suck her nipples for the rest of the day he would do so, and then ask if he has pleased her, with no thought to his own orgasm, no matter how hard he might get.

But she doesn't have all day and pulls him off of her after twenty minutes or so. "Draw another sketch of me before you go off with Tanner, my slave." Darkstar hands him his sketchpad and pencils from her bag. "Make me beautiful."

He obeys, drawing quickly in the sun, and she smiles and adds the new sketch to her collection, noting how prominent her nipples appear in this picture.

"What is Tanner scheduled to teach you today?"

"Flamenco dancing." Jack rolls his eyes.

Darkstar frowns and slaps away his hand that has been resting on her knee. "Attitude, Jack, attitude. Act 'as if.' Did I not give you a mantra?"

"Yes, Mistress." He repeats it: "Everything is possible. I have not begun to open my gifts. I have no clue yet what I can do. My Mistress exists to drag me up into the light where I belong." He pauses and then finishes with enthusiasm, "Everything is possible."

"Good boy. Write it a hundred times for me tonight. And, let's face it, if a guy like you can learn the flamenco, everything *is* possible."

A Gaudi Extravaganza

Darkstar's house is decked out with tiny red lights across the entrance arches, an entrance distinguished not only by the parabolic arches, but by rich ironwork, stone trees, and mosaics of broken ceramic set in the concrete pathway. Inside, red lanterns shine on the stone walls; red satin cloth flows across the tables and drapes from the high ceiling. The decor is a mixture of neo-Gothic and Art Nouveau. Darkstar fits right in—she is standing at the door greeting friends dressed in a long, tight, red spandex dress that is split on both sides all the way up to her hips, the better to show off her black leather sandals that lace up to mid-thigh. She wears a heavy, ornate, black jeweled neckpiece that covers her collarbones and comes to a point in her cleavage, suggesting a modern-day Cleopatra.

China pauses in the entryway while Jack introduces her, delighted by everything she sees. If there's one thing Jack has become since she first met him, besides the love of her life, he's become a little boring and unsurprising and conventional, except when he's flirting with other women to boost his ego, which is still an unsurprising and ordinary pastime. She often wonders if they have switched roles from the early days when she was nervous and scared of her imagination, unable to even imagine working as anything but an accountant, and he was a free and wild soul. China wears a white lace sleeveless summer dress that slips slightly off her shoulders, belts tightly at the waist and ends high above her slender knees. She wishes she owned the sexy, exotic lace-up sandals this woman at the door is wearing.

Jack takes her arm. "China, this is Madelaine Penafiel, my . . . employer here."

Darkstar laughs. "Excellent, Jack. I'm delighted to meet you, China. Do call me Darkstar — everyone else does. I believe I've seen you when I've been in Boulder. It would be hard to forget this lovely red hair." Darkstar reaches out and twists a finger around China's long waves, directly above her nipple, holding her hand there just long enough for China to feel a jolt of electricity, the sensation of surprise in the air, a night starting to fill with possibilities.

"Your home is quite striking, Darkstar."

"Thank you dear, but I only rent it occasionally from a friend for a month at a time. It does have a lot of space, because not only do I like to have parties, but sometimes, on very different kind of days, my two grandchildren visit me here."

Jack does a double take.

"Yes, I have a grown daughter almost China's age who lives in Los Angeles with her five-year-old twin daughters There are so many things we don't know about the people we know, aren't there, Jack?"

Darkstar takes China's arm and leads her toward the kitchen, leaving a surprised Jack with his camera around his neck, his expression mixed between disbelief and amusement.

"Jack tells me your fantasy is to marry him, China. Is that true?"

Safely in the kitchen away from Jack's ears, China begins to laugh. " You're very blunt, Darkstar—it's one of my favorite things in people. But, marry him? You're kidding."

"No, dear, that's what he's told me. And, yes, I'm blunt. I made it one of my goals in life after I left the practice of law to speak nothing but the truth for the rest of my days."

They sit at the big oak island table in the kitchen drinking wine and watch two women cooking, both of them wearing white.

"Not marriage, no. I'd like Jack to be more honest with me, I'd like him to bring me more enthusiasm and spark, I'd like to share my life with him in some way for a very long time, but I believe marriage is an outdated institution, and historically it was never romantic in the first place. I was raised on a commune, believe it or not, Darkstar, and I find I'm actually coming back to a few of their values after all. I want to expand my horizons constantly and live in a natural state of desire."

"Well, tonight may help, dear. If he didn't get your fantasy right, should I assume Jack didn't tell you this is to be an orgy tonight?"

"An orgy?"

"Well, that's the old-fashioned word for it—we tend to call them pansexual piñata parties when I'm here in Spain. Tell me, if he had told you this, would you have come?"

China's laughter fills the room and is contagious to the other women entering. Soon they are all preparing food and drinks and China is chatting away and laughing like she's known them all forever. Darkstar understands that by not answering at all and by drinking more wine and moving in closer when Darkstar wraps her arm around her and lifts her long hair and kisses her neck softly, China has indeed given her answer.

China Is Not a Fragile Dish

More than a dozen women wearing white can brighten up any room, even one as dark as this, Jack thinks, as he sits at the baby grand piano playing tunes and awaiting his instructions from Darkstar. The women lounge around the living room, drinking, kissing, talking, laughing and completely ignoring the only man present. China has wandered over to him once or twice to share her drink or to chat for a minute, but she hasn't said a word about what's going on.

Darkstar sits very close to China most of the time, draping a protective arm around China's bare shoulders while looking directly at Jack to make sure he's paying attention. He is—he's vaguely aware that there are a lot of attractive women in the room, and normally he'd be undressing them all with his eyes, if not his hands, but all he can see now is China enjoying herself, so close but so very far away from him.

Darkstar silences the women, stops Jack's music, and begins to speak. "When I was very young," she says, "I put myself through law school selling cosmetics. It was an American company run by a dynamic woman who taught me an important lesson. Every person, she said, has a flashing neon sign over their heads that says one thing—MAKE ME FEEL IMPORTANT. Her theory was that if you remember this one fact, interpersonal relationships become a breeze and you gain remarkable personal power. It worked." The girls all laugh, even China, who doesn't have the same insight into Darkstar's power that the others have.

"But I learned over time that everyone has at least one other flashing sign right behind the first, and this second sign reveals each person's deepest darkest need. If you can decipher that second sign, well, then you own the person."

More laughter, and Darkstar pulls China onto her lap and strokes her hair. "China is new to us tonight, and she is astonishingly open and trusting here. Jack," she continues, beckoning to him across the room, "take a picture of this moment." Red dress on white, white skin on red, red hair on white—he captures it all, seeing China through a new and different lens, a lens that clearly shows Darkstar's hand resting well underneath the hem of China's white skirt.

"I know what my sign says," Darkstar says. "DO AS I SAY." Laughter throughout the room. "And I know what Jack's sign says—TELL ME WHAT TO DO." China raises her eyebrows at this. "And Patrice here—hers says, SPANK ME LIKE A LITTLE GIRL, and Francoise's says, I AM THE DYKE OF YOUR DREAMS. But China—China is ours to discover. I don't think she knows what her sign says, and I don't think Jack knows either. But he will."

The women move out of the room toward the Jacuzzi in the open courtyard behind the house, discarding various pieces of clothing as they go. Several of the girls gather sex toys, and Jack is offered a drum to play as he follows behind, watching. Darkstar sits China on the edge of the tub and removes her dress, briefly admiring her lacy white teddy before stripping this off too. China sits calmly, her legs hanging down into the hot water, while Darkstar disrobes, enters the Jacuzzi, positions herself between China's legs, and strokes China's clit.

"Talk to me about sex, China."

With plenty of wine under her belt, China says, "Well, Jack taught me a lot in the beginning. He taught me tantric sex and to be braver about masturbation and to be comfortable in my body. But then . . . "

"What, baby?" Darkstar asks, spreading China's legs wider and sliding a finger inside her. Her affectionate tone sends a shiver down Jack's spine. Several other women stroke China's thighs as she talks. Women are in various poses in and around the tub, loving and stroking, but Jack can't even see them.

"That feels so good . . . then . . . then he stopped. Like partners do all too often. His imagination went elsewhere." China turns to look directly at Jack just once. "And he's forgotten that I've barely begun."

"Kiss me, China," Darkstar commands, pulling her down into the hot swirling water, wrapping her legs around her back. The kiss begins and begins and begins again, and Jack can't decide which one he's more jealous of and it becomes unbearable, but he can not seem to close his eyes.

Darkstar finally breaks the kiss and wraps her hands in China's hair with their faces nose to nose, Darkstar's gaze boring into China. "Tell me, China, now. What is your fantasy?"

"This," she whispers, breathlessly. "This. New people, new experiences. A woman. More than one woman. More than one man. Being safe within Jack's love, but being able to experiment and fly. The intensity, the attention, the passion. I've been so good for so very long."

Darkstar smiles over at Jack who hasn't missed a word. "Join us, Jack."

Becoming Bad

It is written on the body that touch is the least specialized of the five senses, but when five sets of hands are touching the skin at one time, the body knows every word ever written. Jack sits in the water behind China, as directed by Darkstar, supporting her beneath her arms, her head resting near his chest as he gently strokes her hair from her face. One woman kisses her, another concentrates on stroking and pinching her nipples, another holds her feet up in the water and strokes her calves while Darkstar takes command between her legs.

"She'll come for me as many times as I want her to, Jack—watch. I know this girl. She reminds me of myself when I was younger, with lust running about an inch below the surface at any given moment, just waiting for release. That first time I saw her with you at a restaurant in Boulder, I knew I had to bring her here—it was more than the red hair—I think it was the way she ate her noodles. Do you have any idea what you have here?" Darkstar strokes China to orgasm once, then again, and Jack merely nods, beginning to remember some things he had almost forgotten.

"Yes," China murmurs, to no one in particular. She

turns her head and kisses Jack firmly on the mouth, drawing him into her, pulling him into her experience. "Yes, this is a good thing," she says to anyone listening, which is everyone by this point, and, "yes, yes, yes . . . " she says to Darkstar as though she has been asked many questions.

"China has been chosen to be our token virgin for the night, our sacrificial slut for the dungeon, so to speak." A murmur of agreement among the girls, all of whom have had the pleasure of their turn at one time." There are few experiences quite so fine for me as to look into the eyes of a novitiate who has realized that my dungeons truly do exist."

Jack smiles—he remembers well the night after his best behavior back in Boulder when he had finished painting his first portrait of Darkstar with her whip, finally earning him a trip to the Green Dungeon beneath her and Tanner's house to hang the portrait on one of its emerald velvet walls. In the dungeon, there were rewards and there were new incentives, all of which were written on his body, and not merely by touch.

When China is laid out on the side of the tub to be dried off by the girls, Darkstar tells Jack to decorate China's body. "Something beautiful," she says. "Make her a surreal walking mural, worthy of hanging on the walls of the Dali Museum." Jack begins to draw with the paints offered him. He draws a sunflower that starts around one breast and flows down to her clit; he draws a garden of the kind that she loves, full of wild colors and flowers upturned to the sun; he draws the night sky running down her arms and abstract waves wrapping around it all. When he stands back to look at this work, he is reminded that China is one of the most naturally beautiful women he has ever known.

Darkstar sits China up and fastens tiny gold clamps with bells on her nipples, pinching each one an extra time when China cries out, caught between the pain and the pleasure that runs straight down to her pussy. Darkstar talks to her, holding her, telling her what she exists for tonight: "To be fucked, dear. To be photographed by Jack. To watch. To test your senses. To perform for us. To go under and still to ask for more."

A full-length, white velvet hooded cape is brought out. China is wrapped warmly in the cape and walked toward the big locked oak door at the side of the courtyard. Jack unlocks the door with Darkstar's key and holds it open for all the girls who parade by him down the stone stairs, some wrapped in short capes, some in leathers, some still completely nude. Jack stays naked and very hard, but no one seems to appreciate his offering.

The dungeon is entirely and blindingly white, even though it is lit only by one lantern on each wall. A pedestal stands in the middle of the room; Jack lifts China upon it.

She stands in awe at this vision of purity, pure white accented by the silver chains and whips on the wall and what looks like a wooden stockade reflected by the mirrors in every corner. Darkstar climbs up behind her to remove her cape. China lifts her hands to the ropes hanging from a hook over her head before Darkstar can even tell her to, willingly accepts the silver bar that is attached between her ankles, spreading her legs wide, and can't stop smiling when Darkstar steps down to admire her work and says, "Welcome to our White Dungeon, China. First, you watch."

China begins to watch things she had never even known existed. Women of all different body types, all looking extraordinarily sexual and beautiful, touching each other: kissing, kneeling, hurting each other and sighing with pleasure. Two girls tie the short, plump Patrice over a white sawhorse and spank her harder and harder in rhythm until she is calling them both "Daddy" and pleading, "Daddy please spank me harder." In the middle of it all is Darkstar, clad in nothing but her silver boots, circulating, touching, commanding, occasionally pausing to slap China's bottom with the riding crop she carries, but saying nothing. Jack is at Darkstar's side taking pictures when so instructed, his hard-on harder than China has ever seen it, and China herself is dripping wet down onto the pedestal until she can stand it no longer, and she says in the loudest voice she can find, "MY TURN."

The girls remove China's bonds and take her down to her knees on the stone floor, circling around and letting her lick their clits, patting her head, pinching her clamped nipples, fucking her face with their hands in her hair. Darkstar moves in closer to her and places a silver blindfold over China's eyes. "You will never know now, dear, just who is fucking you."

Laid out on her belly over white rolled futons, China becomes lost in her own submission as fingers and toys and cocks of various sizes and shapes tease her and enter every part of her, one at a time, then two, then too many to count. She thinks she feels Jack's hands, and maybe he's the one spanking her bottom so hard, but this doesn't seem to matter—pleasure is all there is. When she is lifted up to ride one cock deep in her pussy as another enters her ass, she can hear Darkstar and Jack murmuring in rhythm together, but the sensation of finally being fucked and fucked and fucked again envelops her until nothing remains except the sweet chaos of unrestrained lust.

"I believe," Darkstar says many hours later as dawn is breaking over the Mediterranean Sea and Jack is serving her coffee as she reclines in the king-sized bed, China curled up sound asleep under the quilt by her side, "that this girl's sign just may read *The Official Slut of the New Millennium.*

What do you think?"

Jack laughs, newly able to see Darkstar as more than the woman who controls him, and China as more than the woman he's supposed to be committed to. "She was pretty amazing."

"Amazing? She wanted to try out every damned device I had. By the time we got out of that dungeon, Jack, you and I couldn't even keep our eyes open, and the girls were all worn out. I'm going to sleep for about two days, and then we're going to plan many more China nights. You know what your assignment is when you leave here. You'll tell her everything."

"Yes."

Footsteps trail down the beach as the couple walks home, the sounds above them a sea of laughter. On the horizon of the clear blue sky, just above China's still-tangled mass of red hair, Jack pauses for a moment to read the words that say quite clearly, *"Everything is possible."*

Sex Quest

"Let the beauty we love be what we do
There are hundreds of ways to kneel and kiss
the ground."

—*Rumi*

*T*hey say it is written on the body that only three things make people happy in life and all of them are free —work, friendship and love. If I knew who the hell "they" were who always say these smart things, I'd have to point out that the fine print on my body says—"Annie Braverman begs to disagree—what about sex? "

Of course, when you're on a vision quest in the mountains—alone, trying to be a tough new millennium kind of babe, keeping your matches dry and your spirits high—sex isn't always the first thing that comes to your mind. Or at least it's not supposed to be. I'm supposed to be on a quest for my "issues"—exploring little things like honesty and happiness and my future with my lover, Sam, and the crisis and separation we're going through. There are four other men and women out here in the woods in their own private spaces, and somehow I know that when we gather again on Sunday evening to tell stories like we did the first two nights, they'll all have figured out world peace and I'll have nothing to report but orgasms and fantasies. I also suspect that nobody else even thought of bringing their vibrator as the requisite offering for the campsite altar—bring something cherished, the brochure said.

Probably nobody else brings their Ben-Wa balls into the wilderness either—or do they? This is my undying curiosity—I want to ask every person I meet, "So, are you obsessed with sex like I am?" I do ask this question, in a way, as part of my naturopathy practice, where I serve as a kind of natural-remedies/holistic physician, but of course I ask it politely and with a purpose. When I come to the part in my initial two hour interview with a new client where I say—"tell me about your sex life," they are often shocked, but once I explain how intricately sex is woven into our tapestry of physical, emotional and spiritual health, I usually can't shut them up on the topic. The old saying that "Two things show on a woman's face—not enough sex and not enough sleep" is true for both men and women, but it's also true that it shows in how we live out our days. The most common answers I get to my query, unfortunately, are along the lines of "Don't ask" or "It sucks" or "I used to have a sex life," and age and gender don't seem to make much difference.

This is my first "vision quest" up here in the mountains behind Boulder. After a great deal of preparation—a week of quieting my mind, turning off television, paying attention to dreams, keeping a journal and taking part in the opening storytelling—the goal now is to spend two days and two nights completely alone in my chosen space, pup tent up and sleeping bag on the ground. I don't know, I like my own company fairly well, it's the company of all these other creatures that concerns me. I love my cats—in fact, I wish they were here to keep me safe—but anything that howls louder than they do or creeps silently on the ground scares me to death. I'm trying not to be a wimp, but I can think of so many things we need more of in this world: sexy Argentinian tango movies, great red dresses, white Persian cats, erotic poetry, Navajo beaded earrings, just for starters, and I would prefer that certain other things be removed from my universe forever: yappy dogs, bigoted people, television-wrestling and big black hairy spiders.

I sit on my chosen rock in the bright sunlight, hiking boots on, very high socks pulled up to my knees. I'm wearing khaki shorts and a t-shirt. I've got my dark brown hair pulled back in a ponytail, cheerleader style, but had to leave my favorite skirts and makeup at home. It's time to begin—to meditate or fantasize, these are tough choices. With the Ben-Wa balls tucked away safely in my pussy for now, and few supplies other than water and crackers, I have nothing before me but forty-eight hours in which to think, imagine, get in touch with my inner-self, and be paranoid about the forest. I'm beginning to wish I'd hidden the vibrator in the bottom of my pack after all.

They say we tell ourselves stories in order to live, and on this point I'd agree with "them." The first night's assignment at the campfire was: tell a story about your coming of age or a loss of innocence. One of the men, my friend Doug who talked me into this whole thing in the first place, told a story about turning thirteen and how on that fine day twenty years ago his alcoholic mother handed him a box of Ritz crackers for a present and wished him happy birthday. "She barely knew I existed. I could have been a heroin addict as I went through my teenage years," he said, "and she wouldn't have noticed." We all sat around the campfire as the sun set and cried for him. He talked about his sexuality and his partner, Bill, who is HIV positive, and the joy they have known together for ten years, and his story was enough to open everyone else up.

So I offered the story of one of the few moments I can remember of my childhood, having gratefully blocked out most of it a long time ago. My story wasn't completely about sex, although I suppose all interesting stories have some element of our sensuality in them. I stood up to speak and walked around the fire, unable to look directly at any of the listeners. Staring into the flames, I tried to send my spirit back to that place and time so I could tell the story right, and suddenly I was there and knew again exactly how it felt to be turning thirteen and finding my first lust with a boy named Eddie. I remembered how strong and safe I had felt in my newfound sexuality until the disaster that followed my very first orgasm.

Eddie Winchester is in my math class and he's cute. And horny, like almost all the boys in seventh grade. Me, I look like a "nice" girl, flipped-hair and all, except for the miniskirts that I roll up high whenever I leave home, as soon as I get around the corner. But I have curves on my body that make one of the older boys holler at me one day after I pass him on the sidewalk, "Baby, you have hips made for fucking." I don't know exactly what these words mean, but I think I secretly like them.

During a slow dance at our junior high school sock hop, Eddie asks me to "go steady." All the boys wait for the slow music so they can press up against the girls when the chaperones aren't looking, press themselves so tight against you that you can't help but feel their hardening cocks through their jeans. No one ever speaks of these things. All we know as girls is that we hold some kind of power, and it's scary, but we love it. We think we invented it, because surely our housewife-mothers don't know the first thing about this kind of power. Not that we'd ever ask them.

Eddie and I spend afternoons locked away in his basement, his mother cooking upstairs while we play pool, listen to the Rolling Stones, and make out. Mostly we make out. Eddie can kiss me for hours. No boy's ever done more before than press his lips together and kiss me briefly, back in sixth grade. Somehow Eddie knows exactly what to do—to open his mouth, to suck on my lip, to use his tongue in my mouth, to kiss me until all of my resolve to be a good girl disappears into the music and the taste of our kisses, and I will let him do anything he wants.

He never says anything except, "Annie, Annie," but that's enough for me. I like being adored, being craved, making him crazy. I like being touched. Nobody in my own home ever touches anybody and I want to be touched this way forever. He unbuttons my blouse. I tell him not to but he does, and I never stop him although I know I can. The sight of my white A-cup bra makes him even crazier. Will I let him take it off or make him touch me through it? Will he keep kissing me this way if I let him unhook it? We always keep the bottom half of our clothes on, but on this particular afternoon he lies on top of me on the sofa and begins to grind his hips into me as he kisses me, and I think I will die of happiness.

My bra is unhooked from behind. This is Eddie's eternal quest: to unhook my bra and set me free, and his hand sliding underneath my back feels so good that I don't even protest. My little red skirt is raised during the grinding and there is a lot of skin showing between the top of my kneesocks and my panties. His hands are everywhere—on my nipples, on my thighs, in my panties. He never stops the kissing and the grinding, and I can feel his cock against me, and when his finger slides fast down my panties and up inside me for the first time ever, I am suddenly grinding back against him, my arms wrapped tight around his back, and it must be my voice sounding so much older than my years saying, "yes yes yes," and I know every secret of the universe and nothing, nothing in my young world matters more than that he hold me right there and keep his finger high up inside me.

I don't have any idea what a female orgasm is, but I do know about boys, and I am always pleased when Eddie finally comes inside his jeans with that out-of-this-world grunting that sounds nothing like the stupid things boys say in real life. We lie there afterward, music rolling over us, his mother walking around upstairs, until finally we sit up and rearrange our clothes. We look at each other in embarrassment. He kisses me quickly one last time and then he whispers the words I never hear from anyone: "I love you."

A week later, the week before my thirteenth birthday, Eddie says he has to talk to me. We go to Ford Field after school and stand behind the big triangular slide, a popular make-out spot. Eddie looks as serious as my father does when he's mad, which is most of the time. "Annie," Eddie says, "Annie." He does not kiss me. He does not touch me. "Annie," he repeats as though he is in agony.

"WHAT?" I know he doesn't like anyone else.

I have so much confidence. I know he's crazy about me. I am wearing the cheap gold necklace he gave me when he asked me to go steady.

"Annie. Annie. I went to confession on Saturday. I told the priest everything. He says I can't see you anymore. I'm sorry."

"WHAT?"

"He says you're the kind of girl they call a slut, Annie."

"WHAT?"

"Yes." He pauses, and then says loudly, "My priest said that you are a sin."

Eddie walks away from me and leaves me standing under the slide, tears streaming down my face. I hate him. I hate him, but . . . maybe he's right. I did like it, and maybe that's why "they" call girls like me sluts.

Eddie chooses not to go to hell for me. There is nothing between us after that: no words, no more discussion, no one to talk to—just the craving in the night for that touch once again. I never mention this drama to a soul, and proceed to turn thirteen craving love and absolution, but my family's not even religious, never mind Catholic, so boys will have to do.

They say that events that happen at puberty hardwire your sexuality for life, and "they" may be right again. I thought of myself as a slut every single day of my adolescence. As a grown-up with two children, I still do, only now I embrace the power of the term and know what to do with it. It has been a long strange trip weaving from promiscuous to good girl and back around again more than once to reach the point at which I am satisfied with my work, my friends, my ability to love, and in living out my life with sex and kindness as my religion.

I have survived the first day alone in the wilderness thinking about these things, with nary a big spider in sight. But dusk is falling, and the absence of human voices creates an overwhelming silence, even though I know I can radio the base camp and talk to the leader any time I want. But what would I say? "I should have brought more sex toys. I miss Sam. I'm a wimp. I hate bugs. I'm hungry. Can I go home—I don't want to search my soul anymore?"

Instead I pretend I am a Lakota tribeswoman like the ones our vision-leader told us about. These women wouldn't have crackers, never mind a tent. If a Lakota woman has a "sickness of the soul," it is treated with native healing rituals, but if the sickness persists, she may undertake a vision quest in a power place, clothed in only a blanket and with a little water to sustain her. She will sit inside a circle and wait, often up to forty-eight hours, until a vision comes. This vision could be a deer or a butterfly, or maybe two dragonflies doing battle. All of her fears will come to haunt her and she will face them alone, without radio transmitters or cell phones. When the woman comes down from her quest, she is often said to glow, and her steps will be light, as if she is floating.

It occurs to me that I will soon be glowing with mosquito bites, so I crawl into my tent and zip it up carefully, take off all my clothes, untie my hair, shake out my ponytail, wrap myself in my sleeping bag, and start to run my hands down my bare body while I run my biggest problem through my head. Sam. "Let's take a break from each other," we agreed, as though we were teenagers dating. It was my idea, after I met one of his old girlfriends and learned too many things about him that he forgot to tell me during our two blissful, yet ignorant, years together. I was being a complete hypocrite, since I've kept him in the dark about parts of my life, too. I realize after telling my teen story at the campfire that this may be my big problem with men: I can master the sex, the laughter, the love and the passion, but I can't let them all the way in for fear that they might leave me standing alone under the slide with tears streaming down my face.

I've always thought of Sam as a hero. He is strong and smart and ethical and he cares passionately about investigating all the wrongs of the world. He sat down next to me on an airplane several years ago by chance, and I can remember how my heart skipped a beat when he turned to ask me what I was reading. He was tall and dark-haired and wearing dark-rimmed glasses, and he looked at me as though he knew me. I clearly remember his laugh and what he said to me after I showed him my textbook on natural remedies: "All that new-age stuff is hogwash. Facts are all that matter." Never being too fond of facts myself, I've been working on him ever since.

But it wasn't facts we went for on that half-empty red-eye flight—it was sex. I had been in only semi-slut mode for a long time, cultivating men as platonic friends, carefully choosing normal boyfriends, and sometimes even dating without sex. I was concentrating more on raising my adopted kids and growing my practice than fulfilling my own needs. As our flight took off that day, he put my book away for me, the lights went out, and we talked. We talked about travel, San Francisco, Boulder, and then sex, in quick succession. He was a man obsessed with sex and willing to admit it, so what else could I do? I told him my new life philosophy—that I held sex and kindness as my religion.

"Preach to me," he said, and he reached his arm around my shoulders and pulled me to him and began to kiss me, and I thought the kiss would never stop. It was just like being thirteen. I was wearing a black long-sleeved leotard and a long black-and-red print skirt with nothing underneath and he slipped the leotard down my shoulders within thirty minutes after I'd met him and wrapped his coat around me. I am sure there must have flight attendants on that plane, but I don't remember them and I don't think they tried to serve us any food. There was only this man who seemed to know me, and he just kept kissing me and touching me and then my head was in his lap under the coat and I was sucking his cock and it felt like I was home.

I've always thought the bathrooms on airplanes were designed with great intimate fucking in mind, because you have to get so very close to fit two people, and you have to look in the mirror and see yourself and your partner. There is no way to avoid having the lights on and there are only two or three different ways to position yourself and that is all. Sam stood behind me and bent me over the sink with my face inches from the mirror and lifted my skirt and he entered me from behind with his hands wrapped in my long hair and he whispered dirty words in my ear as he drove into me. He called me a slut and he called me beautiful and he called me wild and he called me his little girl who just needed to be fucked, and he was right in everything he ever said. We finally came together, and then he sat on the tiny toilet lid while I curled up on his lap and he held me so tight that I never quite got my breath back until much later when we started all over again under our blanket back in row 10.

He followed me home to Boulder and stayed for a week. I pretended I'd known him for quite a while—my kids and my friends adored him, we had sex three or four times a day, and the man even knew how to cook. Like the song says, "It all seems so righteous at the start/when there's so much laughter and so much spark." We got the sex and the passion exactly right from day one, but we left out so many important things. Now there are too many secrets and we can't go on this way—I'm quite rich, for one, which neither he, nor anyone else in my life knows, a sort of stupid way to live. Sam despises people with money, just on principle. And then I have this lengthy slut-history, which he doesn't know but surely must suspect. And then god only knows what secrets he's kept from me.

Maybe we need to start telling each other our stories in order to continue to live. Maybe. But I can't imagine he'd be too thrilled to hear how I used to suck men's cocks under the tables in a bar in the LoDo district of Denver. A lot of men. And not for money. They say that practice makes perfect, and I must have sucked close to a thousand different cocks in my life, so I'm damned near reaching enlightenment.

I went to college in San Francisco for a year after I escaped from my family in New York. I stayed celibate by choice that entire year, but the city seemed so gloomy and unfriendly to me then that I woke up every day debating whether to go to class or to jump off the Golden Gate Bridge. Depression was another thing nobody ever talked about when I was a kid. Eventually, I jumped on the first Amtrak train out of town and ended up in sunny L.A.. I worked as a waitress, I frowned at men to keep them away, I took a few classes, and then after six months there, out of the blue, I inherited the money.

It made me laugh for weeks and pulled me out of my unhappy self-obsession for a while. My Uncle George, who I'd only met three or four times before he became estranged from the whole family and moved to Europe, my Uncle George, who had put his hand high on my bare knee when I sat on his lap, died and left me all his money. Millions. Every other relative was cut off and insulted in the will. It was that kind of a family.

I spent tons of money in L.A.—I was used, abused, taken advantage of, and there was something about having a new gold card that made me promiscuous again like I was in high school. Everybody wants to sleep with a rich girl. After being asked for money one too many times by a man who claimed he loved me, I hopped another Amtrak and ended up in Denver.

With my name changed and the money carefully hidden away and cared for by an advisor, I went back to work as a waitress in a popular tavern, wrote sad poetry, continued college classes, and hung out at the bar all hours of the night every night. It seemed like a good plan. I was probably only half-crazy. I died my hair blonde, I called myself a slut—openly, proudly, wildly—an eighties kind of riot grrl, I suppose, ready for anything. Everyone in the district called me LoDo Annie, which I liked a lot.

I began to service men for free. It started innocently when one man bet me I wouldn't blow him under the table, so of course I did and told him to give my winnings to charity. The word spread, there were other teases, and I started my unending practice of sucking cock. My life developed a sound rhythm for the first time ever: get up late, go to classes, write poetry in the park, waitress in the evening, suck cock the rest of the night, go to sleep, start over again in the morning. I gave poetry readings sometimes at the bar, I went off on a few adventures, but mostly I had lots of sex all the time. I was an equal opportunity slut—I'd do the same for women as for men if they were kind to me, but there weren't as many girls around who were eager for a quick licking under the tables.

I didn't have safe sex. I didn't even connect these two words. Everyone was so kind to me, and with everyone touching me every which way I could finally feel like I was living in my own skin. I woke up every single day feeling like sex, and that was all that mattered. When I look back on it now, I'm struck by the fact that nobody, not once in all those years, ever asked me why I behaved this way. They must have had me pegged as a natural-born slut.

I finally graduated from college, did a mini vision quest at dawn at Red Rocks one day, and decided to change my life once more. I disappeared from Denver, went off to grad school in Boulder, and stopped having sex with anyone but myself for exactly two years.

There are animals in these woods that I don't want to meet. I can hear them. I know they are watching me, this would-be nature-babe hiding in her tent, guzzling water and reviewing her life in a search for the truth. I know that I've slept a little and that it's almost dawn, and I'm wishing the animals would go out for coffee or something so I could get up and pee.

I unzip the tent and look out. There are no creatures to be seen, so I crawl out naked, answer nature's call, and then realize that standing in the sunlight in a forest clearing without any clothes on is intensely erotic, and I think maybe I should remain this way for the rest of my quest.

I climb up onto my contemplation rock and lie back in the sun. I can meditate in this lazy fashion for a very long time. After a while it begins to occur to me that our bodies are fascinating no matter what they look like and I think we must be meant to be like this—free, open, sexual whenever the urge strikes, following our instincts rather than our minds. I spread my legs wide and check to make sure nobody's around, even though I know these spaces are chosen for their seclusion. I look down at my body in wonder. I do have hips made for fucking, and what a blessing this is. I started waxing all my pussy hair off after I met Sam, which isn't exactly natural, but is sexy. Maybe I'll grow it back. Maybe not. Maybe I'll stop shaving my legs. Maybe I'll never cut my long hair ever again and see how long it can get. Everything seems possible and interesting and new. There are animals in these woods and maybe I should meet them after all. Maybe they know all the secrets of the universe and I'm not paying attention. Do animals ever masturbate? I don't have any idea, and I like to think I know all there is to know about sex.

I touch my clit with my right index finger and it seems like the most magical spot in the world. Why do we have clits? What a great idea our bodies are. I touch my clit with one finger, then two together, gently, not touching any other part of my body. My two fingers are rubbing back and forth in the sunlight and I feel like a creature of the forest and right here on my body I have everything I will ever need for my happiness. I do not need work and I do not need friends and I do not need love—all I need are food and water and sex. My clit begins to tingle and my favorite sensation starts its run from clit to pussy to toes to heart and brain. My entire body melts into the sun, and I am nothing but heat and light until I open my eyes and turn my face away from the sun, and a visible shiver takes over the warmth when I can't help but notice that there is a wolf standing ten feet away from my face, looking at me as though I might be his next dinner.

He's a deep gray and he's beautiful. He looks into my eyes and I look into his, which are glowing green. Suddenly my danger signals shut down and all I'm thinking is that I love Sam and that's all that matters. This is probably not the smartest thing to think when face to face with a wolf, but it's all that strikes me—the beauty of the moment, the power of my stillness, the realization that animals know exactly how to live their lives. Who ever heard of a wolf on a vision quest? Sam is the man I want to spend all the rest of my days with. This idea terrifies me more than the wolf when it flashes through my brain, but then it grows brighter and brighter until it's as bright as a star-filled Colorado mountain night, and I can't see anything but that idea and the clarity of what is possible. Sam can share all my money, or we can give it away and live in the woods, it doesn't matter, as long as I am with him. He loves my sexuality and he will understand my past. I know what to do. I've been obsessing over all the wrong things. I always wanted to be a woman who runs with the wolves. I begin to laugh at the purity of my thoughts, and it is like being a little kid again and laughing until you want to cry. The wolf takes one last long look at me, and I swear he rolls his eyes and shakes his head before he turns and runs quickly away, leaving me in tears of joy.

"There are no gray wolves in these mountains, Annie," Doug explains to me as we sit at the final campfire back at the base camp, and I just laugh.

"Ha. Nobody knows what is true. We only see the things we focus on."

He nods without arguing as he usually would. Maybe it's the glow on my face that was apparent to everyone when I reappeared. I am a woman who kissed the ground and rewrote her vision of life before she left her sacred space, and that is surely not a woman to mess with.

"So, Doug, darlin', I suppose you came up with a plan for world peace, unlimited funding for medical research, and still had time to discover new flora and fauna?"

He smiles. He is the kind of competent guy who could probably do all this and more.

"OK, OK, but before you even begin to brag, Doug, I gotta warn you. I've got big ideas of my own, and you and all of our good friends are part of them. But I can't tell you about it until I call Sam and see him."

The final storytelling begins at sunset, and I am focused and ready to hear every word. They say the world is made up not of atoms but of stories, and I believe that some day science may just prove this to be true. I say that there are now five things written on my body that will make me happy—there is work and there is love, there is friendship and there is sex, and then there is Sam—and I know these words to be true.

The Seventeenth Woman

*T*he Eaglecrest High School Golden Reunion starts promptly at six on Saturday night and they've asked me to speak. People always think that I am a wise man because I'm a famous author. Nobody thought I was anything in high school but what they call a "geek" nowadays. When I look in the mirror every morning I often still see the face of the fumbling kid that I was—awkward, bookish, shy, and scared; wearing thick glasses; afraid to talk to girls—but now I see that kid through such old eyes. There is a routine required for a man like me to start my day, and it is often more important than the first cup of coffee—I look in the mirror at my aging face and my graying hair and I tell myself out loud, "Leo Graham, you are still young. Paul Newman is older than you are. Sean Connery is older than you are. Women think those guys are hot. They are old. You are not."

But I remember being young in high school quite well, painfully well. The final question on the reunion bio sheet asked, "What do you know now that you only wish you knew when you were younger?" Such whimsy coming from a reunion committee, when all the other questions are so factually nosy (they don't actually ask, "how much money do you make?" or "are you anybody important?" but they might as well.) I could lecture for hours about the things I didn't know back then. I have seen two hundred seasons in my life since high school graduation. Two hundred seasons. Fifty years. It seems impossible. I have loved too many women—maybe I'll tell them about that. Every one of women is still painted in bright colors in my memory, or at least the conquest of them and certain parts of their bodies are. I have been unfaithful to my wife. I have been crazy with lust, wild with lust, head over heels foolish with desire, almost suicidal over women that I barely knew. I foolishly spent all my money on all the wrong things, should I tell them about this? Perhaps I'll just tell them one truth—that I have been in love with Patti Kennedy every single day for over forty years during all of this, and I only wish that I knew then how much this could matter to me now.

The facts of my life read so well on the surface. Leonard Graham: self-nicknamed Leo in college (because I thought I was such a lion); Professor Emeritus of Romance Languages and Literature (because after high school I learned to use my geekiness to make girls swoon from words); father of three grown children (whom I barely helped raise)—two daughters moved out of state and married, one son, whose beautiful wife, Nobeko, just left him (and who could blame her); grandfather of six; world traveler; and author of five books on language and passion throughout history, including the surprise pop-cult hit *The Book of Love,* which has been in and out of print in six languages for over twenty-eight years.

How I wish I had understood when I was younger that the color of a woman's hair can make you want to have sex with her although you know your wife is waiting at home and her hair is even prettier, but you can't remember it and anyway she'll be tired because of the children so, why not? That the glint in a French woman's eye that says, "I know of sex" is enough to take your hormones places you never planned on traveling to. That a man can compartmentalize reality from street-lust and that there is no way to explain this to his wife. Most of all, how I wish I had understood that women have an aura of power that can make a man like me do incredibly stupid things, probably because once you have been a high-school outcast, there is nothing, nothing quite so powerful as the desire to drive your cock home into every pretty woman who wouldn't have given you the time of day when you were young.

But I am a fortunate man. Patti Kennedy will accompany me to the high school reunion Saturday night. I am also a concerned man. I know that Patti Kennedy will be the sexiest woman in the room, and that she will be the only one who knows that I am not wise but rather mostly a fool, and there will be other old men present who would do anything for her. She will wear a low-cut white dress and she will flirt and she will make sure that I know exactly how fortunate I am that she is still with me.

Her name is really Patti Graham, of course, Mrs. Leonard Graham, but she will always be Patti Kennedy to me. I thought I was quite the ladies' man when I met and married her, and I thought she might keep me on the straight and narrow, but she turned from the lovely Patti Kennedy into a mom so thoroughly within the first year of our marriage that I barely set foot on that path. I lost track of her after the children started being born, and I could hardly see her except as a helpmate and housekeeper. She gained weight, she dressed like a mom, she was busy, I was busy. For twenty-some years I mostly ignored her as a woman—then the children moved up and out, Patti Kennedy turned fifty, suddenly she got hot, and now I can't keep my hands off of her. Who could have guessed?

If she had disappeared back in my lazier days, I probably couldn't have even described her to the police, but I sure can now: 5'2", natural pale blond hair, tiny feet and hands, red painted lips, and always matching red nails—Ramblin' Rose is the color. She writes it on the grocery list and I buy it for her, because I do anything she asks today. She has kind and knowing gray eyes, a smallish waist, full hips and hard thighs that belie her age from working out so often with our daughter-in-law, but most of all, she has a bustline that pulls your attention away from everything else. The woman defines the word *stacked.*

The first time I saw Patti Kennedy at a party over forty years ago, she was standing in a garden, wet with rain, laughing. She was years younger than me, a college sophomore, engaged to another man. She was wearing a white cotton summer dress, her large breasts straining against the damp cloth, and I could barely breathe imagining my head buried in her chest. I talked fast, took her home with me that night and told her I loved her while we slow-danced in my living room to a scratchy Frank Sinatra record. My only goal was to get that white dress off of her and see those soft, warm, real breasts—there weren't any fake ones in those days. When I slipped the straps down over her shoulders and reached for her nipples, she wiggled in that sweet, giggly, nineteen-year-old shy way, and her dress fell to the floor in a soft white pool around her high heels. I unhooked her bra and buried my lips between her breasts and there was no day and there was no night and I forgot who I was and where I was and I carried her to my bed, making love to her over and over and whispering every romantic word I had ever known so that she could not possibly protest. Six months later she was pregnant and we were married.

My best friend Jerry always had a theory about sex, which we'd talk about every time we went out prowling.

"Do you realize, Leo," he said to me one day when we were maybe twenty-five, "that if you count carefully, only one out of every seventeen women you pass on the street is someone you would want to fuck?"

I laughed, but I doubted it—it seemed more like every other girl to me. We counted. We tested. We traveled around Europe for work and checked every street we walked down. Jerry's rule proved true. Every seventeenth woman, here or abroad, could make my cock hard. I became obsessed with bedding by the numbers, or at the very least getting each woman to the point of saying "Yes." There are words that can make any woman helpless not to sleep with you, and all of them sound better whispered in French or Spanish or Italian or Portuguese. I developed my own form of the piropo, the flirting street-poetry so popular with men in Argentina. A simple *Diosa! (Goddess!)* uttered in astonished tones can easily start a good-looking woman down the long slide that lands directly in your bed.

A year on the visiting faculty of Arts and Philosophy at the University of Naples and the subsequent publication of my *Book of Love* sealed my fate with women. They showed up everywhere—letters in my mailbox, sexy voices on the phone, young ones in the front row of every class I taught during the sixties, with those lovely legs crossing and recrossing beneath their miniskirts, beckoning, questioning, promising. I knew how to say "I love you" in thirteen different languages and I practiced often.

Te amo, Je t'aime, S'agapo, Nagligivaget, I would say. *Wo ai ni, Ani ohev otakh*—they would fall into my arms and I would fall into their beds, and even though I was not particularly good-looking, I could charm the panties off of all of them. I would spread those legs, so many legs, too many legs to ever count—long lean tan ones and short pale plump ones—and I would kiss the inside of their thighs until they would sigh and then I would whisper fuck me in good old English. They would climb on top of me the way I liked, and I would look at the color of their hair and their eyes and watch how their breasts swayed as they tried so to please me while they rode my hard cock. I could barely remember their names the next day, but I always sent them a monogrammed note with a few lines of poetry, thanking them for sharing their gifts with me. Then I would make the seventeenth mark once again in my journal and look in the mirror and see for that moment a man who was powerful and confident and on top of his world.

I was holding much better odds myself than just being any woman's one in seventeen, because of my reputation. I was proud of this then, and pride builds confidence and confidence builds the air of pride that makes you attractive, and of course everyone knows what pride goeth before, but I only wish I knew this back then. I was so puffed up about my sexual prowess that when there was one girl, just one, whom I could not seduce no matter what words I murmured, I made it my mission in life to conquer her. She was a beautiful Italian girl named Marita who worked at the university. She would flirt with me and I would flirt with her and she would flash her thigh at me beneath her red dresses when she crossed her legs, but her answer was always "No."

"You are married, Professor Graham," she would say with a shrug, as though that ever stopped any other woman. She had a boyfriend, but I didn't care—she became hotter by the minute for having rejected me. She had very long black hair that she wore in a braid, and I knew I would die if she didn't let me run my fingers through the matching black hair down below. I foolishly serenaded her with old love songs, I wrote her letters, I kneeled at her feet and begged her to love me for just one night, but she would not. I threatened to kill myself. I could not sleep at night.

I lost the rhythm of the seventeen, sometimes going as far as thirty-seven or even thirty-eight women before I remembered to count.

Marita fancied herself a poet, and I woke up one day knowing how to seduce her. I would write her a book. Not just any book, a book about love and romance and passion through the ages. A book full of the most beautiful words ever known to man in any language, a book full of sexual innuendo and collected erotic drawings and passionate moments and tales. There are many books along these lines today, but there were none then. I was a man inspired. Nowadays, they'd probably file my poor man's *Kama Sutra* under self-help and call it *How to Seduce Any Woman in Any Language*, but it was a great success at the time. People still quote from that book to this day without knowing where their ideas come from. But most importantly, it brought me great success right in my own bedroom.

"To M, with hope and undying gratitude," reads the dedication of *The Book of Love*, and I always pretend that M was my editor at the time, but M was Marita. I gave her the first copy with a personal inscription, then sent her home from work to read it. She came to my door that evening in tears, dressed in nothing but a red sleeveless dress and black sandals, her long black hair hanging loose down her back. "Grazie," was all she said. "Grazie."

I kept her on her knees for a long time that night, telling her what to do, watching her unzip my trousers and take my cock deep in her mouth, quoting from my book while she sucked. I was not very kind with her because she had made me wait so long, but she did not seem to mind. I stripped the red dress from her body and turned her around, leaned her over, placed her hands on the brass railing of my bed, lifted her fine ass in my hands, and fucked her hard from behind. I recall her murmuring something about her boyfriend and how she should leave, but I could not stop. I knew why she had come to see me and I knew what she wanted. All I had to do was feed her more romantic lines and she would spread her legs wider and whisper "Yes," and I would be back on her like an animal in heat.

She came to me almost every night for a week. I had dreamed for so long of my total conquest of her, inventing an entire new life for myself in her arms, so I devoured every inch of her body each night, pretending like I knew her just because I knew how to fuck her right. I thought she was the goddess who would finally save me from myself, the woman who would wake me up every morning as the sun rose by flinging that long black hair across my legs and lowering her full lips to kiss my cock. It seemed a good dream. She would make me a new man.

It was an appalling time in my life now that I think about it. I wrote my "greatest" work in order to get laid. But for that one week in that dark room in Naples with my cock finally buried deep inside the elusive Marita as she murmured "grazie" over and over again, it's hard to know who was truly more grateful to whom.

The last evening she stayed the entire night and I woke up at dawn staring at her and wondering who she might be. When she woke she looked back at me the same way —still, there is always sex to try and bridge the distance, even with strangers at dawn. We were young and we were energetic and we made love wildly for the rest of the morning, trying to reach each other. I kissed her sweet nipples one last time when we were exhausted and done, but I'm not sure that we both weren't peeking at the time on the clock rather than each other. When she went in to bathe, I stood on my balcony and began, once again, to count the women walking by.

The next day I sent Marita my standard monogrammed note with a couple of lines from Yeats, left town shortly after, and that was the last I ever heard of her.

Patti Kennedy was home raising our children during all of this—trusting, caring, ever-patient. I was faithful for a while, loving her the best I could, but eventually went back to my counting and carousing. It was never quite the same after Marita, because I suppose somewhere down in my soul I knew what I was and I knew I was looking for salvation in the wrong direction. Still, I lived out too many more of my days eyeing every woman I saw who might pass me with a flash of bare tanned shoulders in a summer dress. I would begin to dream that she would be the one, the one with that glorious female form I would conquer once again, and then I would finally know that I had touched a true goddess and I would be a transformed man.

As the years passed, I began to realize that I was getting older and slowing down a bit in follow-through, and the women weren't at my feet anymore. The numbers began to reverse—I was starting to worry if I was anybody's number seventeen at all. There is a great value in staying married for a long time— at least it guarantees you're 1/17 of somebody's sexual attraction.

"Nobeko's coming over, without the grandkids," Patti Kennedy says to me after dinner as we sit with our cocktails on our lovely patio looking out on the sun setting behind the Rocky Mountains. "She's going to help me decide what to wear to your reunion."

"Tell her I recommend a turtleneck," I mutter hopelessly, and I can't believe I say these kinds of things at my age to my own wife.

She just smiles at me. "No, dear, we'll be shopping for something beautiful and sexy and quite expensive."

I'd complain the way a husband is supposed to, but we both know she can afford it, no thanks to me. I made a lot of money from my books, but I could barely balance a checkbook, never mind keep track of where it all went. Patti was always struggling to keep our household afloat when the kids were young, but when she turned fifty, she didn't just get hot, she got smart, smarter than I'll ever be. She started investing what we had in the stock market, took a few classes, got herself on the Internet, and now, at the age of 58, she's at her computer at 7 a.m. sharp every weekday morning—online trading, she calls it. I have no idea what she does or how she does it, but I pretend that I do, and the result is that I never have to worry about money again.

Nobeko joins us for drinks on the patio and we talk about the grandkids, the garden, the news of the world, and then Nobeko's shaky status as a recently-separated single mom. Dear, sweet Nobeko. She's kind and a good mother and I know that she's suffering from struggling with her relationship, like everyone in her generation seems to do. But she's also gorgeous—thin and dark and exotic looking—and I never had any idea why she married my son Jeremy in the first place. I've always hoped that it wasn't because Jeremy's father wrote *The Book of Love,* but I never had the nerve to find out. When she left him a few months ago, Patti and I took her to dinner to tell her that she would always be a daughter to us no matter what happened. Neither of us said that we liked her company better than our own son's, who seems to live in a very cold and detached inner world—a parent doesn't get to say these things, but sometimes you see who your child has turned into and recoil in horror that maybe a good part of the way he is was somehow your fault.

Patti and Nobeko start talking about marriage and separation and affairs, in that open way that only women get to do.

"In our day," I chime in like an old guy, "people left each other all the time. They just never went any further than the sofa . . . "

They both laugh at me, but I do believe there are advantages to not talking everything to death, to not confessing all. God only knows what I would have done if Patti Kennedy had ever put me on the spot during my thirty years of carousing. I imagine that I wouldn't be here in the lovely home this lovely woman has made, relaxing on a perfectly lovely evening with the privilege of listening to the depths of women's conversations. I lean back in my chair and try to imagine myself somewhere else, but all I can picture is a lonely old man sitting on the beach in Barcelona staring at the pretty girls and not one, not one in seventeen, not one in a hundred, not one in a thousand, ever glances his way.

"Affairs," Patti says to Nobeko, "don't have to be the end of a marriage. Look at us. Remember when I turned fifty and called you up and asked you to help me get in shape, and we started running together? Well of course it was because I had started having an affair, yet Leo and I are still happy together."

"What?" I say, suddenly wide awake.

"I said we're happy together, Leo, Isn't that true?" Patti looks at me with a sparkle in her eye.

"Oh, of course! Happy. Yes, indeed." I sit up straight and watch her, but she is holding Nobeko's hand and doesn't look my way again. I heard it all clearly. Am I supposed to know this? Is this why I started paying attention? My wife had an affair and it doesn't matter? Was it her stockbroker friend? The next-door neighbor? Someone I don't even know? Did I even suspect? I can't seem to remember—is this the dreaded onset of senility? Maybe she's just making it up to make Nobeko feel better? How could she think I had ever known if we had never talked about things?

"But we do understand, Nobeko," Patti says. "People change. Sometimes for the better, sometimes not. I got lucky — I loved Leo and I wanted to stay married to him, so I acted as if he was the perfect husband for many years, and eventually he became what I believed in."

"I don't think I have that kind of patience, Patti," Nobeko replies with a shrug, "But you guys are different. You know each other so well. You're everyone's ideal couple."

On Saturday night, I sit on the bed and watch Patti Kennedy get ready for the reunion. She sits at her dressing table in her white silk slip, carefully powdering her face, happily humming a little tune to herself as I've heard her do every morning of our lives together. I've been sitting on her words for four days. Should I ask her now? Will there ever be a good time? Who? When? Where? How often? Were you in love? Why didn't you tell me? Do you still see him? I don't suppose that I'll ever need to ask her why. But, how can I ask—she never once asked me.

"Leo," Patti says, turning away from the mirror to face me, "You must stop staring at me like that all the time."

Of course. We are grandparents. We are senior citizens. She said we are happy. We are long-married. I am just a dirty old man. I used to look at all the women this way, now I save my gaze for Patti. I look at her and wonder: How did she get so young, or did I just get old? What can I do to keep her completely mine?

"Look at you what way?" I ask innocently.

"Like you've never seen a breast before in your life," she says, laughing, walking over to me, and sitting on my lap on the bed. Her thighs are covered in silk stockings and she is wearing garters like the old-fashioned girl that she used to be, and there are places where a man's hands belong whether you've known a woman forty minutes or forty years. I bury my face in her breasts and run my hands up between her legs and find the warmth and the wetness that I need. She is sighing like a young girl, but she has always been a young girl to me, strong and sweet and true—this is what I choose to remember. I must make this woman happy. Perhaps I will write her a book.

But I will start by worshipping her here and now in the way that matters, lifting her up and laying her out on the bed, raising her slip, spreading her wide, lowering my lips between her legs. There is form and there is function and there is beauty, and nowhere in the world does it all come together more powerfully than in the secrets hidden between a woman's thighs. I bury my head there, wrap her legs up around my shoulders and begin to kiss and lick and drive my tongue home, bringing her to orgasm once and then twice and then one last time for good measure. I think that if I can just stay right here and make up for everything I ever forgot to do in all the hours and the days and the years of my life, I will indeed die one happy old man.

"I'd like to introduce our most famous alumnus, Leo Graham. As everybody knows, he wrote *The Book of Love*."

Wild applause and cheering. I look out over the banquet hall—I haven't seen most of these people since the twenty-fifth reunion. I had prepared a long speech, and it was witty and sophisticated and way over most of their heads, often the best way to come off sounding wise. But the first thing they did when we arrived was to present a slide show of high school photos. There I was, in living black-

and-white on the big screen: gawky Lenny Graham, a guy who looked like he could trip over his own shoelaces just walking down the hallway. In spite of my credentials and my beautiful wife and my expensive Italian suit and shoes and the great sex I had just before coming here, I am right back in high school—awkward, tongue-tied, a complete geek standing at the podium with nothing to say.

I consider counting the women in the room. There are about sixty couples—it's odd that nobody comes to these events alone at our age. There are some younger second wives, so I scan quickly for the three out of sixty women who should at least be able to distract me with a touch of eroticism.

There is only one. She sits alone at a table off to my right, shining up at me in the lovely white brocade dress that makes her resemble a bride. She is softly tanned and stylish, and thanks to her cleavage, I've already had to watch every guy at the reunion drool over her and attempt to dazzle her with their stories. She is all I've ever wanted—a naturally elegant woman with an authentic presence, a heart bigger than anything I've ever deserved, and a certain brilliant sanity that will keep me on my toes every day I'm alive.

I find a way to begin: "I was going to lecture you all about life as though I know more than you do. I don't. I know a great deal about chasing the colors of love down through the night, but then, so does everyone our age. I'd say we're all just damned lucky to be here tonight. There is a kind of magic in surviving this far. Renoir, who painted the most beautiful images of women, but none so beautiful as my own *Diosa,* my *Goddess* Patti Kennedy, said, "The only things that are important in life are those you remember.""

"All I can remember now is that I want to spend the rest of my days making love to my wife in every possible way. Love—what else is there? I believe there is a new book of love to be written and rewritten on the very same pages every time the sun sets, and that, my friends, is all that I know now that I wish I knew a very long time ago. Good night."

Dance Naked

*E*very morning I wake at dawn feeling half-crazy, unsure of who I am and what's going to happen next. No one would ever expect this of me, since everyone thinks of me as "wise" Ruby Blackwell, therapist and astrologer extraordinaire, solver of all manner of problems with a flick of my insight, the woman everyone looks to for answers. But the truth is that I am as crazy as the next person, if not more so, and I must reinvent myself each day into the person I've chosen to become—through rituals, through dreamwork, and most importantly, through touching Nita's strong body.

When I turn to her in our king-sized bed, I am always surprised to find her there, sound asleep with that little frown showing in her dreams, the frown I try so hard to remove. She has been next to me every morning for so many years, yet I still delight at the privilege of finding her there. After I write my dreams of the night before in the notebook I keep by the bed, I begin my favorite morning ritual of worshipping her body. It's not exactly a tough task—Nita is an athlete and has a Goddess body that should be immortalized as a statue. This is a woman who makes you want to take your clothes off and go dancing in the rain—an act not uncommon in our house on our better days. We couldn't be any more different physically, though—I am short and soft and plump and rounded in every place she is not, yet we fit together like two missing puzzle pieces that meet at last.

I gently pull the quilt from her body and watch the streaks of light from the rising sun flash across her belly. Nita has many tiny piercings of silver and diamonds and rubies all over her body, and at the break of dawn she sparkles like a crystalline jewel box, the prize at the end of a treasure hunt. Long hard legs with the kind of muscles that I'm not even sure I own, boyish hips and waist without an ounce of fat, nice small breasts, prominent shoulder blades, short cropped black hair—every inch of her looks perfect to me. I start at her toes, stroking, kissing gently. *There will be no alarm clocks for you*, I told her a long time ago since she was so obsessed with rising early and running. *Nobody should awaken so harshly. I promise to awaken you each morning by kissing you into being.* She didn't complain.

Nita's body is a safe space for me, one of those places where you know you belong. This spot here, the little indentation on her kneecap, this is a safe space and needs extra loving. A spot higher up, the spot where her muscles stand out so on her inner thigh, this is where I definitely belong. I carefully caress around her cunt, disciplining myself so that I don't wake her up fully yet, moving on to her hips and her belly button encircled by jewels, pausing for a long time when I get to her nipples. Women's nipples, yes—sometimes I think they are the reason I'm a lesbian. I used to consider myself bisexual, was even married briefly and had kids, but . . . women's nipples. I knew men who were sensitive there, but not like this. The size, the shape, the softness, the fullness in your mouth when you're sucking ever so gently on them, this is a moment to be savored. There is nothing like it, unless it's *this* moment when I gently roll Nita over on her side and watch her sleepy face bury itself back in the pillow as I pause to admire her ass.

It almost makes me want to try to be an athlete myself, just to look like this. I love all body types, including mine. I like being full-figured, and I like taking up so much space in the world. It is unfortunate that while the Japanese have a word for beauty revealed by age: *shibui*, we tend to have words for things like having shapely buttocks: *callipygian* —yet Nita is surely the reason we have such a word. When I begin to kiss and stroke her in that spot just above her cheeks, that spot that is so deeply indented on a woman like Nita, I begin both to lose control sexually and to become fully myself in that moment. This is who I am, this is what I know: I am a woman who loves women, and I am the lifetime partner of the breathtaking Nita de LosReyes, and in knowing this I am the most powerful woman on earth.

Or least in Boulder . . . at least for today. Today I will make things happen. I begin to remember that I have helped plan a party for tonight at Annie Braverman's Blue Room, a party that we've billed as a "Bring a Surprise" party, because so many of my friends seem to have new things they want to share. Nita doesn't know my surprise, I don't know Annie's, and I can't imagine all the others, but the surprise I have to offer is one that will last a lifetime, not unlike the kisses I am laying up and down the back of Nita's legs before I begin to spread them wide with my hands and slip one finger inside her cunt, searching, circling, feeling her hips begin to rotate, trying to decide which of so many ways I might choose to love her awake this morning. There are mornings when I play macho and strap on one of our many cocks that stay hard forever and fuck her in a missionary position with her fine legs riding high over my shoulders; there are mornings when I make love to her only with my lips on her clit forever until she begs me to stop; there are tantric kind of dawns when a full body massage is all that matters; and there are days like today when nothing will do but to keep her face down, prop a pillow beneath her, and fuck her in the most primal way known to wo/man.

I get her favorite dildo out from the bedside drawer, the big, long, curved white one that we both agree looks like no man we've ever known, and position myself between her spread legs, leaning back a bit so I can watch her curved ass move as the dildo slides slow and hard up her cunt, my other hand caressing her clit. She is so wet—her eyes are closed but I know she must be awake. It is our game, it is our love, it is our own private magic to control each other this way, to reach out and listen and love and laugh and cry and fuck each other into another reality every chance that we get. Her hips move in rhythm as I slide the dildo in and out, and I straddle her leg pressed up against my own cunt, prepared to come with her any time she is ready. I am now fully sane, fully alive, a happy woman, prepared to fulfill my lover once again and then again, and then later tonight I will surprise her with something brand new, because I know that the secret to a rich life is to have more beginnings than endings.

"Let there be peace on earth, and let it begin with me," my little family recites, holding hands around the breakfast table before we dig into our oatmeal and fresh raspberries and Nita's freshly-baked muffins. I make them do this—it's what I tell anybody with family problems—eat together at least once a day, say some kind of grace while you touch each other, talk about your dreams, and the patterns of your life will change.

"Well, I think I know what Annie and Sam's surprise

will be tonight, now that they're back together," offers Cara, my fifteen-year-old wannabe rock-and-roll star. "I think they'll announce they're going to get married." A hopeless romantic rocker, that's what this girl is going to be. Maybe it's because her father let her play with Barbies when she was little, those Barbie dolls that they now say could circle the world seven times over if they were all laid end to end. But we also gave her trucks and Legos and music and truth and passion, and somehow I think she'll turn out OK.

Whitney Lee, my twelve-year-old wannabe Olympic snowboarder, snorts at the idea along with me. I have no idea whether my girls will end up loving men or women or maybe both when they grow up, but in Whitney's case I'll be happy if she learns to love anything besides sports.

"I don't think so, Cara. Annie's not the wife type," I say, patting her hand, "but it's nice that you imagine that for them."

Nita rolls her eyes at me. It's funny what the word "marriage" will do to people. Such an outdated institution, yet it still evokes such tradition and romance. Nita looks hip and young, and I look like someone's mother, yet she's quite conservative and I have almost no traditional desires.

Cara just laughs. "Oh, Mom. Just because you and Nita aren't married, and Dad and Doug aren't married, and, well, OK, most everyone we know is not married, some people have weddings and live happily ever after."

"Name some." I shouldn't do this, not at our peaceful breakfast, but I'm a fanatic about reality, and I want my girls to look at the world with their eyes wide open. Being a therapist does not promote warm feelings toward marriage. "And don't forget that the word 'wedding' comes from the word 'wed,' which was the money or cattle which the groom gave to the bride's father as proof of his purchase of her."

"The Grahams."

I knew that was coming—Leo and Patti Graham, everyone's favorite old couple who seem to adore each other after forty-some years. They should bottle whatever they've got and I could sell it out of my office for serious money. "Who else?"

"Oh, well, you know . . . lots of people." Cara looks to Nita for help, but Nita has gone to the refrigerator for more juice, probably on purpose. Once a long time ago she wanted us to get married. We made plans, but then I vetoed them in favor of a vacation in San Francisco, which seemed a much better use of our limited funds.

A long pause, then Nita returns and helps Cara out, looking directly at me. "Besides the Grahams, there are at least three gay couples we know; then there are the Goddards, who we met our first night together, remember? Then . . . Alice B. Toklas and Gertrude Stein—married in Florence in 1910. And then . . . how about Jimmy and Roslyn Carter?"

It seems to me that having to stretch as far as Jimmy Carter pretty much proves my point.

"See? Romance lives," Cara says with a young girl's logic, happy for the moment, then moving on to her next thought. "I'm going to put fake tattoos all over my body for the party tonight, Mom, won't that be a good surprise?"

"Fake, yes indeed. And you Whitney Lee, what's your surprise?"

"I'm going to dress up. Like, in a dress."

What more could a mother want—that will shock everyone. Except she'll probably wear her snowboard boots with it. "And Cara," I say, refocusing in her direction, "maybe Sam and Annie are going to have a baby, or start a new business, or travel, or write a book—don't you think these things would be more interesting than getting married?"

But they're all up and on to their own days and plans, and I've lost them for the moment. Nita gives me a soft sweet kiss before she leaves, laughs and tells me to dream on.

"Always, baby, always. Meet me back here at five without the girls and we'll get ready. I'll tell you then what our surprise for tonight is going to be."

She leaves without discussing our dreams from last night, which is unusual for us. I go back to my notebook instead and begin to write out the details of my own dream before it completely leaves my mind:

It is midnight on the millennium, midnight Greenwich Mean Time, since everyone in the entire world had decided to celebrate at the same time. There are parties and there are concerts and there are families and there is dancing in the streets. I am in charge of this event, of course. I can make things happen. There is everything you would normally expect on New Year's Eve, except there is no television because it has been outlawed for the night. This is to be a primal experience, no instant replay available. Jay Leno forgave me, Dick Clark forgave me, but word is that David Letterman is still pouting.

We have decorated the Equator. We had a lot of help around the world, but it was Nita who mapped it all out. There are Barbie dolls laid out head to toe, in sets of seven, wrapping the entire 25,000 miles. Children offered them up easily when I explained what sexism is—who wants to grow up as less than equal?—and then Nita swam around the world to lay them out. Ever since she mastered the swimming part of a triathlon she figures she can do anything. I picked the equator for the Barbies so that most of them would drown afterwards. Barbie is not a girl who can swim, no matter how you dress her up, though with those tits I'm worried she might float forever. But we've decorated the Tropic of Cancer and the Tropic of Capricorn too—Henry Miller would be proud. Cancer got vibrators, minus the batteries. Capricorn got cock rings covered in shiny honey dust. I bet nobody lets these things go to waste after the party. We finished with the International Date Line—you know how easy it is to get carried away when you start decorating—lining it with every kind of cheesecake known in the world.

At midnight everything stops. There is no music and no drinking and no talking, and everyone does exactly as they've been directed—they sit down, cross-legged if they are able, and hold two other people's hands. There is not a sound in the world except for the distant waves washing over the Barbies. For exactly twenty minutes the entire world meditates, breathing in, breathing out, becoming aware, focusing, and when they are done the pattern of life on earth is changed. Everyone stands up at the same time with a smile that looks almost drug-induced and we all remove our clothing.

There are little piles of neatly folded clothes covering almost every inch of every continent, and everyone stands very still until I begin to play my crystal flute. Nita is sure I'll play something spacy and new age when she would have preferred the Rolling Stones. Mick Jagger was not available to help—actually he just wanted too much money— but I know he too is standing naked in London ready for the next moment. As the first note from my flute is heard around the world, each person turns to another and says quite clearly in one of the five thousand languages in the world, "Peace be with you."

And then the dance begins. My song for the night is the old Van Morrison song "Wild Night," which proves that you never really know anyone until they surprise you. The dancing is called peace-dancing, a spiritual kind of dance that takes place even in real life, though usually to much slower songs. Things happen at a heart-level in peace-dancing, because it is an intense ritual. People are required to touch each other, to look in each other's eyes and connect, and suddenly, easily, there exists the kind of intimacy that people are starved for.

Hypnotic waves of humanity are bobbing to the strains of "Wild Night," and fortunately I can hear Van Morrison backing me up, standing there stark naked in Ireland singing with the soul that the world is so in need of . . .

. . . and everything looks so complete, when you're walking out on the streets, and the wind catches your feet and sends you flying, crying . . . the wild night is calling . . . come on out and dance, come on out and make romance . . .

Bare bodies of every type and shape and color are moving through the dreamy intricate steps that vaguely resemble a sexy square dance, and there is a subtle sensual buzz to it all just as I dreamed there should be. There is magic and play in the world and it is so damned important. People just forget to laugh and to listen and to love, and I think I'm on to something here. I know how to get to world peace, and just when I think it can't get any better, the night sky begins to fill with silent sparklers, millions of sparklers, set off by the equatorial Barbies, who are being useful for once. The sky is shimmering silver and the sparklers spell out the words, "hope comes in many forms." I never want to wake up, because I know that what happens next is that all the children will go to bed and every adult on the planet will find someone to make love with in some way, and the idea of worldwide sex and peace and love all at the same time begins to surpass my own borders of joy.

"OK, Annie," Sam mumbles through her kisses, "have you got it memorized?"

Annie Braverman laughs and keeps kissing Sam, wrapped tightly on his lap, locked away in their bedroom, safe, happy, amazed.

"Stop, stop, this is serious, Annie. Money is serious stuff."

She stops for a moment. "Really? I thought it was the root of all evil."

"No, that's just one of those quotes everybody gets wrong—it's the love of money that's the root of all evil."

"But love is better anyway, don't you think?" Annie asks, sliding her skirt up and moving on Sam's lap to get his attention. Ever since she told him that she has been secretly rich for a very long time he's been different in some ways, though at least he's been very happy about it once he got over the shock.

"You're not rich," he had said when she first told him,

in the middle of riding high on his cock, pausing to tease him with a "surprise."

"Yes, I am," was all she could say before they went back to lovemaking. Then she waited for him to bring it up afterwards.

It took a day or so before he questioned what she had said. She told him again, to his disbelief. "Nobody's secretly rich," he said, "that's just something people make up in stories." Finally Annie had to bring out her financial statements to prove it to him.

Sam hasn't stopped smiling since.

"I thought you hated rich people?" she had to ask.

"Oh, I do, I do. Except for you, baby. I'll make one really big exception for you. Do you have any idea what those kind of millions can do in this world?"

Of course she did, but his imagination overtook hers.

"Yes, baby, love is better," Sam says now, giving in to her hips circling on his cock. "But another quote is untrue—love is *not* all there is." He lifts her up and lays her down across the bed. "We only have a couple of hours until this party, Annie, so maybe we can do both here. I will make love to you and you will listen to me while we plan how it's going to be tonight. I know it matters to you, and it's going to matter intensely to other people—sometimes I think you've forgotten how incredibly erotic money can be to people who don't have much of it."

Annie sort of hates to admit it to herself, but it's damned sexy the way Sam has taken over everything for her.

He lifts her skirt and spreads her legs, moaning at the sight of her bare pussy. With each ankle tied loosely to the lower corners of their four-poster bed and her wrists tied over her head, Annie is just about exactly where she wants to be.

"First," Sam says, teasing her clit lightly with his thumb, "tell me the words. Tell me how you'll announce it."

"Ummm . . . " Annie says, trying to remember. "I'll say—I've come into a major financial windfall from a distant uncle who died."

"Perfect, baby. And it's true. Nobody's going to ask how long ago he died, and you never have to tell anyone. And we'll wait until the very end of the night so we don't overshadow anybody else's surprise." Sam stops to brush her hair from her face and kiss her softly. "Good girl." He lifts her light white sweater up over her breasts, leaving it up around her neck, pausing to slowly suck on just one nipple, nipping, biting gently and then a little bit harder. "Oh I like this, Annie, I do like when I can slow you down and get you to pay attention."

"More, more . . . " Annie whispers, so Sam stops and starts talking again.

"More?" he teases. "OK. Everybody believes you. They have no reason to doubt you like I did. As far as they know, you just became a multimillionaire last week. Once you're past the first semi-truth, it's easy. Tell me the rest." Sam's fingers begin to touch her clit once again, but this time there are two fingers from each hand and they are reaching in, exploring, stroking, opening her up. "Tell me, baby."

"Oh, then I just tell them the three points and surprise them. God, yes, Sam, please keep doing that . . . "

"Surprises, Annie, yes. You're the queen of surprises. Here's one for you." Sam's fingers slide in and out, one hand and then the other in rhythm, two fingers and then three and then four, filling her up, sliding in rhythm with her bucking hips, reaching in and pausing to hold her in place and then starting again, driving her crazy with his stops and starts until finally he puts his hands together like he's praying and slides all the fingers from both hands inside of her at once with his thumbs on her clit and he whispers, "Come for me, Annie," and she begins to shake like she will never stop.

He moves up beside her and unties her wrists, holding her tight until she comes back to him. "I like being tied up," she whispers to him.

"I know you do." Sam kisses her again and again, always aware when he's kissing Annie that the lips are the part of the body most sensitive to touch. "And I'll never stop. But there's more to talk about before we continue. Tell me the three points while I undress."

"God, Sam, I have no idea . . . "

"I'll take them for you, baby, if you can't handle them later, don't worry. I know you love the people that will be there tonight and this is hard for you." Sam climbs back up on the bed and wraps his long legs around hers, leaving them tied to the bedposts. "First: we tell everyone to bring all of their bills to your accountant tomorrow. A world-class fantasy for any adult. Second: we tell them to take a week and decide upon one wish and bring it to me—yes, that would be me, not you, Annie, they know I'm tougher. One dream that money could help them obtain. World peace and unlimited riches are not to be included. My only criteria will be the ancient touchstones—is it true? is it beautiful? is it moral? Man, if this isn't erotic to you, baby, you've had money way too long. And then lastly, we'll tell them our own plans, my own fantasy lived out, and how they're included."

Annie feels like simultaneously laughing and crying at the way Sam is and the joy she has been able to bring him, but decides instead to actually ask him for what she wants.

"I have a wish, Sam. And it's free, like most of my wishes." She whispers to him of something she used to secretly dream about when she was a young girl, and then he begins to kiss her in a very different way, and she can't help but notice that there is no more talk of money, just kisses, and desire, and Sam untying her ankles and removing all of her clothes. The look in his eye is exactly right as he gets the hairbrush from the nightstand and begins to run it through her hair and down over her hard nipples. She strokes and kisses his cock and it is very hard, so hard that she tries to think of a way to keep it in her mouth, but he is pulling her around and bending her over his knees as he sits on the side of the bed, and when he begins to spank her bare bottom with the hairbrush while his cock presses against her belly, everything else possible is removed from her mind.

"Yes, Annie, baby, yes," Sam says between strokes on her lovely ass, "you're right, sweetheart. There are some amazing things that money just can't buy."

China and Jack arrive at the Blue Room for the Bring a Surprise party early, bringing a woman I've never met before, which, well, surprises me. "Ruby," China says to me with a secret smile, "this is Saffron. And, no, she's not a Spice Girl . . . she's our new lover."

Now this kind of surprise I like. I look at China and Jack, who I never expected to still be together, and at this young woman named Saffron, who looks like the kind of techno/punk/young/sweet girl my daughters would adore. "*Our* lover?" I ask, even though I can guess the answer that's coming.

"Yeah," Jack laughs a little sheepishly, "China and I have decided to openly practice polyamory, which I think is every man's fantasy." He watches China and Saffron cuddling and flirting.

"Welcome, Saffron," I say, giving her a big hug.

"Saffron works at the Celestial Tea Factory," China tells me. "We met her when Jack decided to help fulfill my weird fantasy of making love in the Peppermint Room."

China is my kind of gal, obsessed with food and

cooking, though you'd never know it to look at her slender body under all that red hair. She's done me a big favor and made a special dessert for tonight to help with my surprise. Everybody around Boulder visits the Celestial Tea Factory sooner or later—because it is a beautiful place, because they give tours, because they are good employers, and because they give great free samples. But the Peppermint Room is a point on the tour most people walk away from—just standing at the doorway of a room filled with nothing but peppermint can make your eyes water with the intensity of the smell. I try hard not to ask constant questions when I'm out of my therapist role, but my curiosity will kill me on this one. We're in Annie's Blue Room, after all, which is built for sensuality and fantasies, so I ask, "Well, did you?"

China laughs and holds Saffron close. "Oh yes—it was fabulous. It was almost like . . . flying. I'll let Jack tell you all the lovely details." I watch the two girls wander through the room, China proudly showing Saffron the erotic books and the fountains, and then they slip behind a Japanese screen while Jack talks to me.

"It was amazing," he says. "At least for them. I had to wear nose plugs, no kidding, which is not very sexy."

Jack is long-haired and artistic and has a reputation as being free and wild, but I suspect that China's new wildness is a little difficult for him. I will not utter the words that come to mind as I listen to him, "be careful what you wish for . . . "

"They spread peppermint all over the floor, Ruby. It was after hours, about two a.m., with the doors locked, of course. Saffron's a supervisor there, though I don't know if she will be for long. China's always had a peppermint fetish, and I never even liked candy canes when I was a kid. But we did it—we're taking turns fulfilling each other's fantasies. They stripped down and put peppermint on each other's bodies and licked it off. I couldn't do it. I took a lot of pictures—peppermint doesn't look like much on film, but China and Saffron sure do. I think they forgot I was there after while—they finally climbed way up on the stacks of the bags of peppermint and I had to scramble to join them. They did this thing with their tongues—China would wet her tongue just right, put a layer of peppermint on the tip of it, touch Saffron's nipple and sparks would fly. Saffron would do the same to her tongue and touch China's clit over and over and the sparks would fly and then China would start coming . . ."

"No sparks for you?"

He looks a bit bashful at the memory. "Ah, well, a few —they got my jeans off and they started stroking me up and down with their tongues and setting off the sparks, licking me like I was a candy cane on Christmas Eve, but I couldn't take it—at first it just tingled but then it felt like I was on fire. I ended up just watching them eat each other and the peppermint until it got close to dawn, and then I made them stop. I'll tell you, Ruby, I had to bathe them both for days to get rid of that aroma."

Seems to me there are worse ways to spend your time than bathing these two beautiful women, but my reverie is interrupted by Nita's arrival. She is dressed as part of our surprise.

There are many surprises presented on and off during the evening, some funny, some consisting of food offerings, some just in the way people appear, some career changes, some surprises told as stories. China and Jack make a formal announcement of their polyamory, which pleases everyone, because China looks so happy. Nobeko Graham announces that she will be officially divorced shortly and is moving into a loft near the Denver Mint, and while her divorce is not exactly a surprise to me, I'm happy for her too. The kids who have all been allowed to attend the party until the stroke of midnight have all dressed to be funny and different, and it is quite charming. I wait a long way into the evening for my own surprise, but I notice that Annie's doing the same thing.

"You first, Ruby," she says to me at one point and we argue it back and forth, because I know that my surprise is going to outdo whatever hers might be. But it is her Blue Room, after all, and everyone seems to be nicely tipsy on the champagne punch that China has provided, and there is a slant of moonlight in the garden upstairs that suggests a little magic in the air, so I figure it must be time.

I bring Nita over to me, get everyone's attention, summon up all of my nerve and say, "In case you're wondering why the normally lovely, tailored Nita de LosReyes is wearing all these flowers tonight, I'm here to tell you. Looking like this is not her real surprise. We want to announce what my grandmother would call in her fine German accent a *hochzeit,* which translates literally into English as a "high time," which translates technically into something that will amaze you all, a wedding."

"Who's getting married?" my sweet daughter Cara asks, confused, looking toward Annie.

I bring Cara and Whitney up with us. "We are, dear, Nita and I. It surprises me too. Everyone knows I married a man, a good man, your father, when I was nineteen, because it never occurred to me that I could marry a woman. But I can. And I will."

She is a good daughter; she does not say a word about cattle or bad marriages.

I look at Nita and she is just smiling through all of this, not speaking, just smiling, but it's a smile that's near to breaking my heart because I know what this means to her. "Some day," is all I would ever say to her after our initial plans for a big unity ceremony got canceled. "It doesn't matter," I would tell her, "it's just an out-of-date heterosexual tradition," and most days it wouldn't matter, except that it always did to her. She never doubted that I loved her, I'm sure of this, but at the end of the day I know in my heart that love is an action, not just a feeling or a bunch of words.

"Wow, Mom, that's so cool!" Cara says, and everybody else is applauding, and the tears in Nita's eyes make me wonder if I've ever really had a single insight in my life before now.

Annie is hugging me, then hugging Nita. "That's so beautiful, Ruby. I was wrong—your surprise is the best. But, when will this *hochzeit* be?"

"Yeah, Mom, when will you get married?"

"Tonight. Here. Now."

The moonlight in the garden glistens off Nita's face and her dress of flowers. I had Nobeko help design the dress, made entirely of white gardenias and baby's breath and orchids over lace. It is very short, the better to show off her lovely legs. I wear a long black crepe skirt and a white satin shirt, and as we move to get ready for the ceremony I am suddenly thinking about very sappy things, like whether I could actually lift her up and carry her over the threshold when we get home.

"We wrote our words a long time ago," I tell our friends, who seem to be sort of speechless, "and even though technically in Colorado a couple can marry themselves, our friend Jerry here has offered to officiate for us. He's had at least a couple of successful heterosexual marriages in his church, as I recall."

I hold Nita's hands and we begin. There will be no invitations, no gifts, no big plan, only the moment and the moment is now. Someday we'll just do it, that's what I kept saying, and I cannot remember for the life of me now why I forgot to follow through. Jerry gives us a formal introduction, says a few words about love being all there is, and then asks for our vows. They are simple, and we say them together. "You are my love, my soul mate, the woman of my dreams. I will stay with you through good times, through bad times, and through all of the days between. You are the reason for my birth. I take you to be my lifetime partner for loving, for listening, for laughing, for crying, and for dreaming. I love you."

There is utter silence in the room, and we exchange the simple silver rings we bought so long ago. I think it must be the moonlight, but Nita is glowing, and so are my daughters, standing a few feet behind her in their tattoos and boots. Or maybe it's the tears in my eyes that make everyone look so shiny and new.

We kiss. We kiss for a long time, a serious kiss, a kiss filled with soul that means something. No one says a word. Finally we stop, and Jerry says a few more traditional words about blessings and love and then he says, "May I present to you Ruby Blackwell and Nita de LosReyes . . . uh . . . " and he fumbles on just what exact version of man and wife we might be, until I offer, "equal partners," the only thing that any couple should ever be.

Nita and I both wear frilly blue garters high on our thighs and we go for it—there will be no bouquet tossing for us. I remove the garter from her leg and she removes the one from mine, to much teasing and hooting. We turn our backs and toss, but I peek over my shoulder in time to see Annie's cat Zenrose jump up high and catch them both midair, and I can't even imagine what this might mean.

"Cheesecake!" says China. Her creation is brought out on a cart—a many-layered cheesecake piled high to resemble a wedding cake, complete with two naked women embracing on top. While we're laughing and eating cheesecake and enjoying the warmth of our friends and I'm explaining to them what peace-dancing is and how they're all going to do it for me tonight after the kids are gone, Annie says she better sneak her surprise in here before we all let loose into the wild night.

Annie's rich, I'm married . . . she's going to pay all my bills, I'm going to live happily ever after. They're going to fulfill people's dreams. Then I think there was something about Sam and Annie and her kids taking a year off and traveling to find the perfect place to open a bed and breakfast, a place based on sex and poetry, a kind of a permanent Blue Room open to the select public. Sam wants to write from there, and we all have free lifetime invitations to visit them wherever they are. Did they really say all these things? It makes me wonder if getting married hasn't addled my brain already.

But I am wearing a wedding ring and there is dancing beginning in the moonlight to the sound of Jack playing his guitar and singing a slow soulful version of "Ripple"—*let there be songs to fill the air*—and I'm still not sure if I'm caught in one of my dreams or in real life as Nita takes my hand and draws me into the dance. There are many hands and there is touching and bodies are spinning around and around, and when China and Saffron begin to undress in the middle of the circle I know what will happen next, and I know that when Nita removes the flowers from her body and begins to touch my face I will have finally found the point at which dreams and reality become one, and I will know exactly the way to take her home.

The Night Flight to Rome

*I*n my dream I am Sam Davidoff, ruler of the known world. All the women in my universe have to climb the stairs and come to me for inspection once a month. They bow. They call me "Sir." I have a big red S tattooed on my chest, which I like to think stands for Sir, or even Sam—not Superman—but it's funny how childhood memories get mixed into adult dreams. When I was a kid, all I wanted was to be bigger and stronger than I was, to save people and punish all the bullies of the world. I might even have worn a red cape if this would have helped. I used to read three things constantly, all with equal dedication—the encyclopedia, the newspaper, and *The Arabian Nights*. When I wasn't having superhero fantasies, I was deep in unruly thoughts about women. *The Arabian Nights* taught me that two things corrupt women—gold and the perfume of saffron—tough things to get a hold of as a kid, but I sure could dream. Never once did I read that talking and communication and honesty were going to be in the mix.

Jack Iverson is my sidekick in the dream. I am the Commander of Clits; he is the proud Priest of Pussies, and he is wearing a cape, a long black one, which he wraps around him to hide his constant hard-on. Each woman climbs slowly up the high circular stairs toward me. I sit in my big armchair, perched atop one of those rare silver-blue night clouds full of shining ice crystals. I am still tall and dark-haired in the dream but I do not wear glasses, because I have perfect eyesight and can see right through women. Visions of the paintings that haunted my youth float behind me in the clouds—Seurat, Dali, Renoir—the nudes and bathers who reclined sensually, having what looked to me in my desperate youth like unending wild days and nights.

There are rules for the women in my universe. They all wear skirts and like to lift them and touch themselves. They all like sex and are gracious enough to share the secrets of what women really want with any man trying to corrupt them. No one is rude; everyone laughs a lot. Not one woman even thinks to ask the question, "Do I look fat in this?" because they are all lost in the magic of their sex and know they are beautiful exactly as they are. And every single woman is not only an expert on tantric sex, but also enthusiastically bisexual.

After each woman bows before me, she lifts her skirt and twirls around, showing off her bare pussy. Jack's job is to weave a single flower into each woman's pussy—calico roses, scarlet begonias, oriental poppies—and then I wrap a single strand of saffron around their clits. It's a tough job, but somebody has to do it. There are no other men available for the task because they are hard at work harvesting the saffron—it takes two weeks of picking through 64,000 crucus sativus flowers to come up with even one pound of saffron—but we men don't mind this work as long as it keeps the girls happy and corrupt.

Jack's always bucking for the clit-wrapping job because I get way more orgasms than he does. A woman stands in front of me in my dream, and this lovely creature looks suspiciously like my Annie in real life, except that she has blond hair. That's the one, Jack whispers to me, the girl I told you about, the new one, the one they say knows more about sex than anyone in the universe. The girl laughs at this and hands me a red rose. She looks a little dangerous. The rose has thorns. I hand it to Jack and he winces. The new girl slowly lifts her long blue skirt, all the way over her head, and she holds it there, covering her face so that I cannot watch her eyes as she begins to twirl and dance in front of me. Her legs are long and strong, her hips undulate like a snake, she has not a single hair on her pussy and she dances with all the motion of the winds but never moves farther than two feet from me. I look to Jack for help, but he is so enamored that he's busy weaving an entire bouquet of flowers with her rose in the center.

Go to Jack, I mumble, as though I am the one in charge, and she laughs again from beneath her skirt and twirls over to let Jack plant his bouquet deep inside her. It takes him a long time, and I watch her body shiver and tremble as she comes once and then again for him as he meticulously arranges each flower. When he is finished, the bouquet is arranged between her legs so that in place of normal pussy hair she has only flowers.

She twirls back to me and stands very close between my spread legs, pressing one knee up against my bulging cock. This girl knows exactly what she is doing. I grasp the outside of each of her thighs and bring my nose to her bouquet. She begins to caress my face with her flowers and I am lost in the sensation. Saffron will be redundant, but I begin to tie some strands together, pry her lips apart with two expert fingers, and wrap the saffron around and around her large hooded clit as she starts coming, leaning forward and putting her arms on my shoulders to steady herself.

I consider tying one last long strand to attach her clit directly to my cock and closing down this cloud forever, but there are so many people depending on me. I lower her skirt from her face, stroke her hair while she recovers, lift her back up to her feet by her bouquet and send her off to the line of waiting women with a swat to her bare bottom.

All the women descend the stairs, riding high on the windhorse energy of sex. As they pass before me on their way down, they each flash me their flowered pussies and I feel like I'm lost in a Georgia O'Keefe painting.

It's the feast of reason and the flow of the soul, Jack says as we begin to close down the cloud. Let the rain fall where it may, we're going to go watch the Cubs baseball game on the nearest satellite.

Cumulus, stratocumulus, cirrus, cumulonimbus . . . I awaken to find myself staring out an airplane window high over the ocean naming all the clouds I can think of. Annie Braverman is dozing next to me, smiling in her own dreams, her long blue skirt pulled down tightly around her knees, her pale blue sweater taut across her hard nipples. I hope these nipples are because she is dreaming about me. I'll have to find out. Surely this is a woman who is in need of my inspection.

I stroke her hand, lift her skirt and reach for the silky spot on her inner thigh that is enough to make me start getting hard. Perhaps I can be so quiet that she'll keep sleeping while I touch her . . .

But she wakes up, smiles, and now we must communicate before I can continue.

"Sam," she says with a yawn, "are you still nervous about the plane?"

There was a sort of unexplained "boom" sound shortly after takeoff that made everyone jumpy. It was nothing, said the pilot much later, but *nothing* rarely goes *boom.* "Oh, Sam," Annie said at the time, "don't worry. My friend

Nita told me once that even if you were born on an airplane and flew every day of your life, you wouldn't approach the statistical probability of an accident until you turned eighty years old." I know about statistics, I fly all the time. This reasoning sounds so sensible until you remember that eighty-year-olds aren't the only ones who die in plane crashes.

"Nope, not me," I say in my best macho guy voice, but I turn and look nervously out the window.

"That's good. Hey, you were dozing when I came back before, but guess who's on the plane with us?"

I think she's trying to distract me. "I give—who's on the plane, Annie?"

"Mister Rogers. He's in row two," Annie answers with a laugh. "I got his autograph."

"Mister Rogers?"

"Yes, you know, Fred Rogers. With the sweater and the kid's television show. Look." She puts an airline magazine in my lap and on the cover it is inscribed—"To my friend Annie Braverman—you are special. Fred Rogers," and there are some strange characters after his name. "That means "grace" in Greek," Annie says. "He's headed to Athens after Rome."

I am safe. Mister Rogers is in the neighborhood and he is Annie's friend. If anybody's got a hotline to God, it must be him. He probably flies a lot—I just hope he's not eighty years old yet.

"I bet Mister Rogers knows the names of all the clouds. Tell me about him," I say, paying close attention to anything that makes her smile like this. We have told each other story after story about our passions and our pasts, but I still half expect Annie to come out with something outrageous at any moment, like maybe she ran off to join the circus once and forgot to tell me that story.

It is dark and the seats around us are empty on the long

flight to Rome. I think I could spend the rest of my days right here, flying the night skies with Annie, excavating her mysteries and her magic. But the best thing about first-class airline seats, besides the service, is that women can spread their legs wide in them. I turn her sideways toward me and move my blanket up around her shoulders. "Lift your skirt for me, Annie, and then tell me."

To hear a woman talk of ordinary things while she sits in front of you with her legs spread, beginning to touch herself—yes, this is one way to corrupt a man. Her feet are bare as she swings them onto my lap and she wears nothing beneath the skirt. Facing me and my window with her skirt up at her knees, nobody in the world would know what she's doing unless they were passing by on a cloud outside.

"Well," she begins, knowing exactly what her curious brown eyes, sly smile and stray tendrils of long dark hair falling down from her ponytail do to me, "I always thought Mister Rogers was kind of sexy when I was a kid. You know why? Because he knows things."

"Things?"

"Yeah, the things that matter—like what children need to grow up happy, why love is all there is, what the real meaning of life is. Those kinds of things."

She begins to tell me these secrets in a whisper while I watch her stroke herself like a kitten. Her fingers slide in and out and circle her clit, almost casually, as though she's just patting her arm instead of arousing herself, and me, past the point of no return.

"I see, Annie," I say, as though I'm paying more attention to the words than to her pussy. "And he told you all this while I was asleep?"

"Yes. And, he held my hand the whole time. I asked him if he'd come to the bed and breakfast place that we're thinking about opening in Italy if he knew that it was dedicated to sex and poetry."

I dip two fingers into her pussy, bring them to my mouth, taste and watch her watch me lick them clean. I used to think you had to get completely wild and over the top to get kinky, but the truth is that all you have to do is get a little weird and creative and intimate and keep sex on your brain all the time. I put my two hands on her knees and spread her legs as wide as they'll go.

"Was Mister Rogers shocked at you, little girl?" I say sternly, as though she is a naughty child.

"Oh, gosh, no! He said maybe. He would bring his wife if he came. They've been married for almost fifty years. He said they're still in love. So, he's on our guest list now." Annie picks up a hairbrush from the seat pocket in front of her and begins to slide the handle into her pussy.

She's flirting with me, teasing me after all this time, and I love it. I don't care if her stories are wild or true or completely invented, as long as I'm the one she keeps sharing them with.

No more words, just Annie in the night with her legs spread wide and a hairbrush handle slipping faster and faster up inside her, one thumb rubbing her clit, my hands high on her inside thighs, watching, waiting, until there is no other possibility but to give her what she wants.

"Annie. Come for me."

The handle almost disappears with the contractions of her pussy and I hold her face and kiss her quickly to quiet her cries. When she subsides, I pull the blanket over my head and take a superhero dive to rescue that hairbrush.

I wrap her back in my arms and watch her fade into sleep once again. Women hold all the secret power in the world—they have all the babies, they have orgasm after orgasm . . . and what exactly do men have that is as special? I will have to focus on this after we arrive in Italy, before the children and a complete menagerie of friends and pets start arriving. This is a woman to worship, and I will. This is a woman who can almost make me see God, this is a woman a man would be crazy not to marry. Except that she won't marry me—she says I can share all her money, help father her kids, travel the world with her, but she doesn't like the way men become "husbands" and forget to be lovers, and lovers is what she wants to be. Somehow I'll have to prove that I'd be an exception. Or maybe some day I'll just tie her up with a thousand strands of saffron and make her do exactly what I want her to do.

I felt like I had fallen into a fairy tale when we were preparing to leave home for a year of travel. I remember what China Thomas said. She's our friend back in Colorado who is so pleased to think of herself as the *Official Slut of the New Millennium* that I half expect her to have it tattooed on her belly next time I see her. "Wow, Sam," she told me, " you must have been surprised when Annie told you about all the money she has now."

Surprised? For almost twenty years she'd been hiding her wealth from everyone she knew, quietly investing in childrens' groups, wisely growing her windfall with socially conscious investments, never telling a soul. Surprised? I'm a journalist, facts are my game, yet I'm still having trouble imagining how much even a million dollars really is, never mind her kind of money. I had to pick up some books on investment just to grasp the concept of owning serious money. One day at the bank I learned that there are no more five hundred dollar bills made in the United States—who would have guessed? Plastic reigns. One Cezanne painting sold last year for sixty million bucks: that's one obscene way to think of money. But I try to keep in mind the Zen theory—if you want to know people's values, ignore what they say, look at their checkbook and their daytimer, and find out where they spend their time and money.

Each of our friends came to us before we left with the one wish we told them we'd grant with the money, after we paid off their bills. Nobody asked for a car or cash, and everyone wanted to promise us something in return. There were requests for education—cooking school for China, grad school in architecture for Nobeko. There were investments in small businesses—Erick Flanagan and Jack went in together on a snowboard shop, and Jack swears he's going to invent the next new thing in snowboards that will let shmucks like me get down the hill without killing ourselves, and thus be able to pay us back with his riches. Ruby Blackwell and her partner Nita wanted nothing. We told them they had to be more gracious and accept a gift, and finally ended up making a donation in their names to an Internet adoption site.

Annie awakens with a start in my arms and tells me she had a weird dream. I could fall asleep and wake to listen to her dreams forever. I spent time in a Buddhist monastery once on assignment, and they told me that there are only four natural states in life in which mind and body are truly one—death, sneezing, falling asleep, and orgasm. I'd prefer to skip the first two and focus on the latter. Sleeping and sex, sex and sleeping, these are some of my favorite things.

"There was a guy who swallowed swords in my dream, Sam, and he was sitting naked in the middle of the desert with me. I actually knew a guy like that once, but this wasn't him."

"You knew a sword-swallower? Where?"

"At the circus. And, Sam, in my dream this guy kept frowning at me and repeating, practice, practice, practice."

"You knew someone at the circus?" I think I'm losing

both time and my ability to speak fluently on this flight. "And this guy wanted you to practice swallowing a sword?"

"Well," Annie says with a smile full of promise and sex, running her hand directly up my leg and patting my cock, "maybe not a sword, exactly."

I take her hand without saying a word and lead her past Mister Rogers sleeping in row 2 and up to the front restroom.

"It's all in the tilt of the neck," she whispers when we're safely locked inside. "Men always get the wrong angle. That's the secret."

She is sitting cross-legged on the floor with her head tilted back as far as it can go and I'm trying to control myself long enough to get above her and gain the right sword angle, which is no small trick in this tiny bathroom. "They never swallow with the swords out in front of them, or lying in bed, or upside down, only like this, sitting down, head back, with the sword held straight down over their heads pointing down their throats," she says.

Finally my jeans are down, my hands press hard against the opposite wall to hold me up, and Annie is polishing the tip of my cock with her exquisite tongue. She pulls me down toward her and I am sliding, driving, farther down into a woman's throat than I've ever been before, and she is only tilting her head back farther and massaging her neck on the outside and pressing against my cock and it is longer and harder and deeper and I catch a glimpse of this in the mirror and there is no other possibility but to give her exactly what she wants, and I do.

Asleep with her head on my lap, I think maybe I've finally worn her out for the day. I will do everything for this woman. I will cook—long leisurely meals at outdoor tables full of friends and good conversation, meals that exist as a work of art. Like Dali said, all good art should be edible. I will write things that matter. I will love Annie and I will love her kids. She will continue to heal people with her life force. We are both going to learn to paint. There will be no more failure of the imagination for me. I will make Annie work on her fantasy of rewriting the *Kama Sutra* for the twenty-first century, which she could probably do with one hand tied behind her back. What else can there possibly be? And in between all of this, we will have masked balls and kinky sex and outrageous dreams, so that things will always be much more than they seem.

What else can I give her? Plenty of sex? Any man can give her that. *Think big here, Sam, think big, this matters.* The plane is starting its descent, and suddenly I know. The scary "boom" at takeoff was a clue.

I'll do what I learned while at that monastery, only modified for sex. Those crazy-wisdom guys were constantly bowing and meditating and praying, all trying to reach the magic number of 111,000: 111,000 prayers, 111,000 full bodily bows, 111,000 mantras. If they reached it, they called it a "boom." It was their goal—you reach enlightenment or something, the world changes around you when you realize you've completed something you thought was impossible. That's it—111,000 orgasms for Annie, a boom of sex, that's the goal. I'm calculating. It starts today. I'm forty-four, and she makes me want to live to at least a hundred . . . maybe four or five a day—man, I wish I'd started corrupting her much, much sooner.

I look down at her sweet sleeping face and try to imagine her face the day, what, sixty years from now? when I show her my secret orgasm tally-book. It will work. She will be mine. If only I could crawl inside her dreams before then and know all of the things that make her smile that way . . .

. . .They call me Princess Annie and I live in a palace on top of a cloud that no one can reach. Still, some man keeps knocking on the big wooden door and asking me if I dream in colors. "I don't know," I tell him, "but I come in baby blue and silver and deep emerald green."

"Does it make you sad?" he asks.

"No. I just stay in my palace of emerald dreams and write about sex as though it matters."

"Will you write about me now?"

"I don't know. Maybe after you've climbed up my stairs and made me come into infinity."

"You can count on me."

I don't know what else to say to this man's voice, so I keep repeating that sex and kindness are my religion, and suddenly I see Sam off in the distance sitting on a weird looking shiny cloud. His cloud is floating closer to mine, and I begin to hop up and down on my cloud like a tiny princess in a Nintendo game. Little gold coins fall shimmering from the sky, the stars begin to bounce, and a giant rainbow appears. I lift my skirt and use my superpowers to twirl from my cloud to his. I think that maybe I have more life points than I can ever know what to do with, and I am falling into paintings and falling into clouds and I am lost in a dream and then I'm riding reality. There is a brilliant sanity to it all and Sam is stroking my hair from my face and telling me we're about to land and I keep mumbling, "sex and kindness are my religion, sex and kindness are my religion . . ."

Two strong hands, touching lips, touching hair, touching skin, reaching home.

"Preach to me, Annie. Preach to me."

About the Author

Susannah Indigo's stories have been published in many anthologies, including *Best American Erotica, Best Women's Erotica, The Mammoth Book of Best New Erotica, Of the Flesh: Dangerous New Fiction,* and in numerous online magazines. She is the co-editor of the anthology *From Porn to Poetry,* the Editor-in-Chief of Clean Sheets Magazine (www.cleansheets.com), and also the founder and editor of Slow Trains Literary Journal (www.slowtrains.com). See her Web page at www.susannahindigo.com for more information.